Fragments from Being

A Short Story and Poetry Collective

J.A. Terry

Pandora's Boox

Some of the events described happened as related; others were expanded and changed, while others are complete works of fiction. Some of the individuals portrayed are composites of more than one person, and many names and identifying characteristics have been changed as well.

FRAGMENTS FROM BEING

Published by
PANDORA'S BOOX
www.pandorasboox.org

ISBN: 978-0-578-03068-5

Printed in the United States of America

Table of contents

"Literature; the most seductive, the most deceiving, the most dangerous of professions."

-John Morley

.

Fragments from Being

.

Louis

Of this world I sometimes wonder; with his built-in adapter that connects to all others.

A most interesting being; whose thoughts spill forth, as fast as the blood rushes his veins.

Words and numbers…numbers and words, a higher level of consciousness, where advanced technology and grey matter infuse; emotion in motion, never stopping, rarely slowing; entertaining the masses while causing commotion, dancing to a beat all his own.

Bound to Leave Her

She knew one day he was bound to leave her
But hoped that his stay would be longer
The fact that he left without a word
Is hardest of all to face
Not knowing what he was thinking
When he simply walked away

Her heart still yearns
Though her mind moves forward
Refusing to look back
But still wavers in moments of weakness

When she walks the night unable to sleep
Memories come alive and invade her mind
Her body responds as her mind remembers
The passion with which he touched her

It can't be love if you don't look back
And though he never said the words
She never had a doubt —

Illuminati

He rose up from the depths of her unconscious mind, like smoke drifting from the unknown, wrapping himself around and penetrating her soul. *"I feel you...I feel you"*, she whispered inside; as dawns early light crept in and illuminated the scene and softly he faded into morning's mist, just as she reached out to bring him to her.

Dysfunction Junction

We looked at each other in disbelief, as the familiar face flashed across the television screen. We then watched in stunned silence as they shoved him handcuffed, into the back of a waiting police cruiser, while the reporter gave details of the latest in a long line of gruesome serial killings spanning three years and 13 states. The phone immediately began ringing and didn't stop for two days.

One could never be certain if she was trying to convince others, or herself, when she described their gypsy lifestyle as adventurous and educational; moving from state to state, staying in one place only long enough to get settled into a routine and familiarize themselves with the area, before bad luck inevitably struck and they were forced to pack up and moved on, yet again.

They prayed about it, as a family, knowing that as long as they had faith and were together, that wherever God led them, they would make it work. But work was what was needed to keep them that way.

Her parents, sisters and brothers all offered to take them in at various times throughout the marriage; wanting only to provide her and the kids some stability and sense of normalcy, while he was off chasing his latest whim; but their offers were seen as offensive attempts to drive a wedge between them. The argument always the same; home-schooling being the best thing for the kids and the bond of closeness unlike any they could find, if they led what others defined as a normal life.

I'd heard the stories but had no opinion one way or the other, as live and let live is something I've always believed; until they came to our area and I visited their campsite and saw for myself, the cramped conditions in the pull-behind camper trailer, in which 2 adults and 3 children lived. There was a lackadaisical attitude when it came time to actually teach the lessons required by those who home school, and it was evident that in no way would these kids be up to par, should they be placed in a regular classroom and given grade level curriculum. But for all intents and purposes, they seemed normal enough, despite the obvious underlying layer of antisocial tendencies; and suddenly I understood what all the fuss was about.

I also identified the cause of their dysfunction, upon meeting and spending time in the company of the husband/father/breadwinner, which held the reigns so tight that no one breathed without first asking permission. It was sickening to watch this thirty-something, overweight, unattractive loser, take pleasure in ruling his roost, as it were, and making his loved ones flinch upon command; using religion and the Word of God as a weapon, or tool, depending on the favored outcome from his subservient wife and submissive children.

But I knew there was more to it and the problem ran much deeper, when his answers were limited and he refused to look me in the eye. And so being the person I am, I went out of my way to instigate him in conversation and watched in silence as he squirmed and grew more uncomfortable by the moment; having a woman speak her mind, give opinions and question him mercilessly. They packed up and left the next day and that's the last we'd heard of them until the news report revealed the secret that had been driving their lives and leading them down the path of unrighteousness.

Admittance

It was the first day of the 40th annual art festival, on the grounds of an historical park that sits along the bank of the St. Johns River and I'd been looking forward to it for days. You see, I'd finally talked my friend Suzanna, who happens to be an amazing photographer, into setting up an exhibition booth and displaying her talent.

I woke to the sun filtering through the trees, a gentle breeze blowing my curtains in soft, billowy puffs and a squirrel chirping in the feeder just outside my window, telling me it was time for a refill. The house was empty, but for me and my little dog, and I rather enjoyed the peace and solitude.

I wanted to get to the festival early, but I couldn't ignore my muse tapping me on the shoulder, so I made myself an espresso and took my laptop out under the pergola and wrote for two hours, nonstop. Apparently I had lots to purge, and so I did…then headed to the festival, with a spring in my step and a smile on my face.

Suzanna's display was beautiful and her tent was already full of browsers and buyers. She'd brought an extra chair, (director's chairs, reminiscent of the ones my parents had back in the 70's), with the hope that I'd hang out with her for while, which of course I did.

She'd asked me once before, what I thought about writing a short verse to display on the matting of certain photos that I found inspirational, but to be honest I hadn't given it any serious thought, until she mentioned it again and gave me one to look at.

I was studying the image as she meandered among the browsers, answering questions and making conversation. I held up the print and spouted off a verse. Suzanna cocked her head to one side, examining the print while digesting my words, and then out of nowhere, his voice rang out above the din of the crowd, wrapping itself around my heart then thrashed it mercilessly against my chest, as I looked up and met his gaze.

"What's that?" Suzanna asked, as she turned her attention to him. "I said, what about morning's mist," he answered, without looking away. "Oh, are you a writer as well?" she asked excitedly.

He turned away and started rifling through a display of small prints and said, "I've dabbled a bit, but I don't know that I'd call myself a writer." She happily announced to him and everyone within earshot, "Well she is, this is my friend…the award winning author and poet…" and trailed off with a list of my books and pen name.

I could feel my cheeks burning pink; not only from embarrassment, but the heat he sparked inside me, and just as I touched my hand to my cheek, he looked at me; unsmiling, but held my gaze for several seconds, until I turned my attention back to the picture I was still holding and not another word was spoken.

Our chairs were centered at the back of the tent, blocking the rear opening, while giving easy access to her stock that was packed in containers behind the tent. And so I sat there, as Suzanna went on to make a sale, totally oblivious to the secret torture I was suffering, while he slowly browsed, making his way in my direction.

I was fine until he came to the end and stopped to admire the pictures that hung to my right, and I caught the scent of him. I kept my head bent, as if still concentrating on the picture I held, my long curls spilling over my shoulders, blocking my face from his view. I closed my eyes, breathed deeply and held it, as if somehow inhaling even his scent would appease whatever it was I felt welling deep inside me. And then I felt him, his hip pressed gentle, yet firmly against my arm.

I raised my head, but refused to look at him, for fear of losing myself in what I might find in his eyes, as he pressed closer against me, like the alpha male that shoulders against the weaker dog, making a stand and taking his position in one domineering motion. So close he was, that I could see the individual threads in the weave of his jeans, and his thigh muscle outlined against the denim. Closer than he'd been in years; than I ever dreamed he'd be again.

I felt the raw, sensual power radiate from him, as my resolve slipped away and he walked around me, reaching out to brush his finger across my lips as he went. Without thought, my lips parted and my tongue instinctively met his flesh; the jolt coursed through my body, as if a bolt of lightening searing its way through to my very soul.

What was this hope I felt building; this invisible force that I succumbed to whenever I found myself in the presence of him? My will no longer my own and my desire...

Then just as quickly as the flame had sparked, it was extinguished; all hope crushed, desire weakened to shame, as he walked past, chuckled deeply, and said, "I don't think so!"

Tell Me

How do I cool my lips, after losing myself in your heated kiss
How do I ease the rush, after melting under your lovers touch

How do I turn away, when our eyes are locked in that gaze
How do I find my way, after you've led my mind and body astray

How do I let go, once you turn around and walk out that door
How do I keep myself from always wanting more

How do I distinguish the need from the want
How do I stop my heart from falling in love –

Esoteric

Intelligible only to those with special knowledge –

As the moon pulls the currents
Your energy flows through me
As the air that I breathe
You are always with me

As the stars fill the sky
Your life-light brightens me
As the river flows to the sea
Your presence draws me

As the mysteries of life
This connection will not be unraveled
As the power of prayer
I find peace in you

As a spirit is illusive
So are you to me –

All that is real

With a single word or touch
He breathed all that was real
Into my world
My eyes were opened
And I thought to myself
Yes…
This is the way it was intended –

When Night Falls

Minutes turn to hours and hours to days
As time ticks on and dormant she lays
Staring with unseeing eyes

Having no conscious perception of what she is seeing
Focusing solely on the dull ache inside
As her heart beats on…keeping her alive

Exhaustion finally claims her
And slowly steals her away
Into fitful sleep…where she cannot escape the pain

Lost moments play in her mind, as a movie in her dreams
Moments that have passed and are over
But that can never be stolen away

Then light comes and breaks the night
Signaling the rising of the sun
Forced to face another day
She wonders if the strength will come –

Falls to Pieces

The sun is setting quickly
And the warmth I basked in
Just moments before
Leaves me cold and unfeeling

A numbness that consumes
From the inside out
But has little to do with the chill
That fills the night air

It's the tearing apart of my heart
As the seam is split
And everything falls to pieces

The severing of the connection
That momentarily
Breathed all that was real
Into my world

Making me feel complete
And whole
Giving me reason to be
Nothing more than myself –

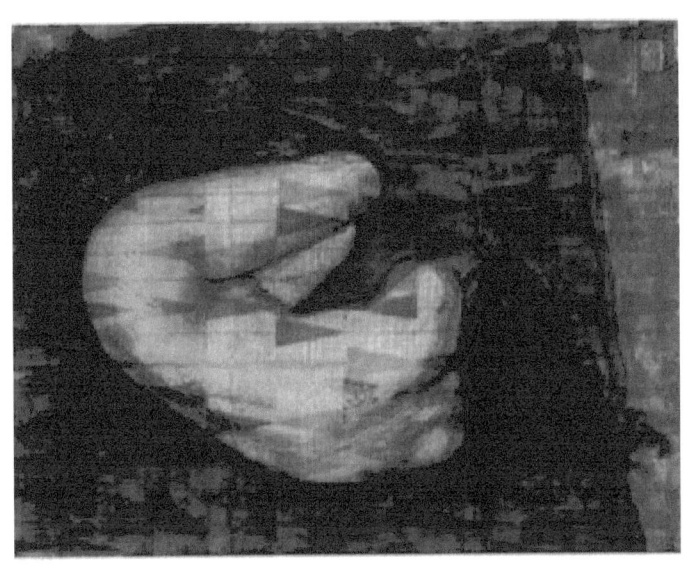

What Lies Within

They say a person is never truly dead, so long as there are those left behind to keep the memory of them alive, but it was the memories that had driven Louis to this point of no return. Not memories of the wonderful times and the love they had shared, but rather the hazy moments preceding the accident that had taken her from him; the flash of bright lights, the sounds of searing metal and screeching tires, meshed with her piercing screams; the overpowering scent of gasoline and the dampened earth, and then there was nothing; nothing but silence, and the blood, so much blood.

The arrow of time had pierced his heart and there was no reason, it seemed, for him to move forward. For the moment she'd left this world and entered another, the life had bled out of him and it was time, he'd decided, to end this misery.

He sat on the edge of the bed and reached for the bottle of Halcion that Dr. Baker had prescribed at Sebastian's insistence. Sebastian, he thought, as his hand tightened around the bottle and he let out a shaky breath. He'd made certain that his Will was in order and that the old man would be well taken care of for the duration of his life. He'd toyed with the notion of leaving a letter, explaining his reasons, but he knew that wasn't necessary, for Sebastian had been with the family for as long as Louis could remember and was closer to him than his own father had ever been.

Sebastian was a gentleman's gentleman, very old school and from a time when wealthy men had personal servants. He offered Mr. Van Ness the kind of loyalty that no amount of money could buy, and so it was only natural that the Van Ness' had named him as Louis' guardian and benefactor. It had been twenty odd years since their passing, and Sebastian had come to love Louis as his own son, but even that was not enough to save Louis from the grief that now consumed him.

He poured the contents of the bottle into his hand and counted roughly twenty-seven little blue pills. He shot the lot of them into his mouth then reached for the glass that sat on the bedside table and washed them down with tepid water. The deed was done and now it was only a matter of time until he was free from the earthly hell he'd been dwelling in.

He walked across the room and stood before the wall of glass that looked out over the city, taking in each and every detail, knowing it would be for the last time. The rain came softly, and although his view became distorted, just as his mind grew weary, still he watched, as life played out before him. He felt a slight pang of melancholy when he realized that the world would go on without him tomorrow, just as it did today, and other than a handful of people who would surely mourn his passing, his demise would not directly affect the balance of the universe.

Strange Magic

It's something that happens whenever the thought of you comes to mind, the sound of your voice is heard or the touch of your embrace is felt. A quickening of the pulse, beating to a rhythm so unnatural as to leave one wondering how life can be sustained at such a rapid pace; yet the body has never felt more alive. The explosion of emotion as it swells to the breaking point, as you desperately gasp to catch your breath, yearning for a moment more...always just a moment more. Then feeling as if a part of your very being has been ripped from your soul, when the connection is severed, and you are left alone to search for that lost part of yourself. Knowing exactly where it is, but having not the means or ability to retrieve it –

The Date

Two brothers, as different as day and night; one athletic, sexy and cocky, the other studious, well-dressed and mannered. I wanted the athlete of course, but the other was the one who asked me out. He was a few years older than his brother, already established with a job and apartment in the city, and I certainly didn't scoff when he made the 35 mile trek to pick me up in his shiny black 911 Porché, (which wasn't so impressive and felt like a VW bug once inside).

He'd decided to take me back to the city to dine at a hip new restaurant that he'd recently discovered. Turns out it was one of the old abandoned buildings that sat along the railroad in an industrial part of the city and it *was* quite the hot spot, considering. The interior had been converted into two separate dining areas with a large bar as the focal point. It was a little louder than I would have liked, but I really dug the vaulted ceilings with exposed beams and duct work that ran throughout, and the brick walls added a warm, cozy feel.

The menu featured everything from Filet mignon with lobster tails to brick oven pizza. My date decided on calamari appetizer and pasta fagioli entrée's. I was impressed that he'd taken it upon himself to order for both of us, as no one had ever done that before, until I realized that calamari was squid (which I have since learned to love) and the pasta had beans in it (which I still hate), so I ate all of my salad and picked at the rest.

The conversation flowed, as did the wine and I was glad that this was the brother who'd asked me out, until he mentioned going back to his place and what a wonderful Sunday brunch the Palm Court in the Omni Netherland Plaza serves. Perhaps I misunderstood, I thought to myself, but no, he definitely intended for me to spend the night, and that's when things got awkward, as I had no intention of staying with this guy.

I acted as though I hadn't heard, as I tactfully picked around the crunchy little beans hidden throughout my pasta and changed the subject, but he pressed the issue. Left with no choice, I politely told him I wasn't the kind of girl who sleeps with someone on the first date and he immediately called the waiter and asked for the check. He then proceeded to calculate the tab and tell me in no uncertain terms, what my half was.

Luckily, I always carried cash; mad money and an emergency stash, which I'd never had to use until now. I counted out my half and threw in a huge tip for spite and then ended up kneeing him in the crotch when he played his last card and politely opened my car door then grabbed me up in a desperate, groping embrace. Asshole!

I took off down the darkened street, pissed off and humiliated, with absolutely no idea where I was going. I walked my way uptown in heels that were made to look good, not to actually walk in, and ended up hailing a cab. The driver looked at me like I was crazy when I told him where I wanted to go. I sat in the back and watched the meter rise with each passing minute and tried to figure how far what money I had left would take me. Twenty minutes later we reached familiar territory and I made him drop me at White Castle, where I went inside and called home then spent my last .35 cents on a cup of coffee to drink while I waited for my mom to come get me.

True story.

P.S. I went out with the athlete brother a year or so after, played an exhausting game of tennis at the club and nearly gagged when he took his shirt off on the way to the shower and the hair on his back was long enough to braid. I made a beeline for my car the minute he was out of sight and left a note on his windshield saying that I was suddenly sick to my stomach and would call him later. I never did.

Rekindled Memory

Sitting in the shadows of the warm Southern sun, the gentle breeze caresses her skin as the song softly plays in the background; rekindling a memory of not so long ago…

She found herself in his arms, lost in a forbidden kiss…filled with answers to every question she ever asked of him. And in that moment there was no place on earth she'd rather be. But as with all things that moment did too pass as the would-be lovers separated and distanced themselves, the memory bittersweet for her now; the breeze playing upon her skin as his kisses once did. Not so very long ago –

A B r e a t h A w a y

Retreating to the safety of the life she knows, gathering shreds of
dignity as silently she slips away. The ease with which he
dismissed her forcing her to go; leaving her to wonder if his truth
was just a lie.

The darkness of an ego bruised pales in comparison to the
emptiness which her heart does feel, even at their darkest hue.

Yet he remains on the outskirts of her mind, always only a breath
away; and still her heart quickens at the thought of him.

Plaguing her always the question…*why?* A single loaded word
filled with every answer her heart does seek and still he holds the
only key –

Death Becomes Her

Jules paced the room until she felt the walls closing in. Strangers scurrying up and down the hall, and the stench of death smelling up the house. She slipped out through the parlor doors that opened onto the side porch to get some air; leaned against the post and took a long drag off the cigarette that was nearly burned down to the butt. She flicked it in the yard and checked her watch, all in one fluid motion; wondering just how long this was going to take.

The neighbor lady and her two kids were sitting on the front porch swing eating their lunch; something they'd never done before; but then they'd never had a show like this before. Neither had the group of gossips that were gathered on the corner. Jules shook her head in disgust; watching ruefully, as they covered their mouths with their hands when they spoke, as if that somehow made their speculation less obtrusive.

A few minutes they wheeled out the body in a dingy black body bag and load her into the corner's wagon. She'd never given it any thought before, but given the given the condition of the bag they chucked her mother in, she wondered if they actually reused those things.

There would be no grieving for Jules. No sadness over her loss and not a single tear would she shed. In fact, she was glad they were finally leaving, so she could get down to the business of sifting through the shit and picking out the stuff she knew she could sell.

No, Jules only had one regret when it came to the death of her mother; and that's that she had died in her sleep, instead of suffering a slow painful death, the likes of which she deserved. One of the officers came round and handed her a clipboard with some papers to sign. He expressed his sympathy, to which Jules gave no reply.

No sooner had the coroner's wagon turned the corner, than the onlookers flocked toward the house to see what they could learn from Jules. They reminded her of turkey buzzards that hang off to the side of the road; one eye on the carcass and the other on oncoming traffic; waiting to pounce the minute the coast is clear.

Jules didn't give these buzzards a chance, as she quickly turned and walked back inside; closing and locking the door behind her. Rumors were sure to spread like wildfire through the little town, as people drew their own conclusions of what exactly had happened to Magdalene Beck, but Jules could care less.

Once inside, she opened all the windows so that the cross breeze blew out the last remaining traces of her mother's death. Now all she had to do was clear out the rest.

She methodically went from room-to-room and removed any and all personal objects that her mother had kept for sentimental reasons, or otherwise. She started with the shrine of portraits; her mother's seven dead husbands; each of whom she took for whatever she happened to need at the time and they had to offer; but not before four of them had taken exactly what *they* wanted from Jules.

No, there would be no mourning for Jules where her mother was concerned, only years of healing and loneliness lie ahead, in that big old empty house.

Clarity

I find it amazing yet daunting, how easily the heart leads us astray. With
its wicked games and fanciful notions; playing upon our deepest
emotions. We follow it willingly, as the sensations that flood our senses
are too powerful to be anything but real. Until the moment of truth
shatters the illusion; leaving us with nothing but fragments of what we
believed it once held and what is revealed in the end amounts to nothing
but pain –

Into the Abyss

For a moment he opened the eyes of her heart and in a single beat the world came to life. The darkness and doubt that surrounded her, suddenly replaced with certainty and light

His luminance was such that she never had seen, drawn to this beacon like a ship lost at sea. The shallows were safe to linger and just be. The depths promised relief from the scorching heat.

With trembling hands and a yearning heart, she breathed deeply and focused before taking the plunge. Not knowing where the tide would take her, but ready for the journey all the same. She closed her eyes on that fateful day; softly she called out his name.

The undertow was fierce, more so than expected, as the waves crashed over she felt as if she were drowning. Many times she fought her way weakly to shore; her body exhausted, her mind unsure. But each time she felt the sand in her toes, believing she had her footing, he shined his light, reached for her hand and eased her back in his waters for more –

Chance Meeting

I rounded the corner and saw him there, head and shoulders above all others. Not due to his height, but the pedestal he still sat upon, which I had placed him

He did not tear his gaze away as expected, but looked directly into my face. Mirrored in his eyes was everything he had glimpsed whilst dabbling through my soul

Each thought a prayer…each act a deed…every day a celebration

And in that moment I knew the purpose of discernment; through experience of what was of true value and what was false; and the acceptance of personal responsibility –

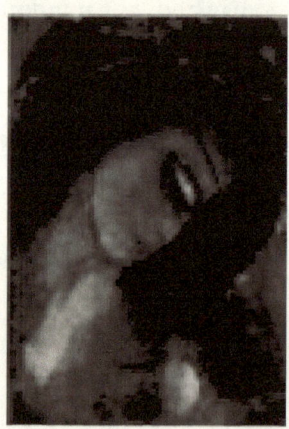

On days like this

I cried for you today; as I drove myself alone in the dark. I could feel you; as if you were touching me that very moment. I was filled with a myriad of emotion. My stomach muscles tightened, my heart gave a little flutter and the tears stung, then filled my eyes.

I could feel your arms around me, holding me in a tight embrace.

Remember turning to face you; slowly you took my mouth with yours. How easily I could lose myself in you.

The flames danced through my body as I leaned into you, longing to be closer; the feel of your flesh against mine; but that moment was enough; your kiss and your touch and always such a sweet surprise. How the sparks they do fly.

Then there are days like this when I can't get you out of my mind; I remember how I felt when you touched me and it isn't enough to simply remember.

The sweet sorrow of wanting you, not being able to have you, breaks my heart on days like this –

The Brothers Grimm

He heard his son screaming across the yard. Horrified, Keith looked up in time to see his nephew, Joshua, with the yellow plastic bat raised over his head, whacking his cousin. Not just once, but four times; yelling in his little boy voice, "shut…the…fuck…up," each word correlating contact.

He reprimanded him immediately; taking the bat and explaining that it was wrong to hit, but even as he spoke, he couldn't help but wonder if all his effort was expended in vain, as he gazed into the child's wild, staring eyes.

****

They grew up in the same upper-middle-class home with the same parents, only 3 years apart in age. They witnessed the same fights, the same violence, the same rage, yet they interpreted it completely different.

Keith, the younger of the two, tried to protect their mother on several occasions, coming out battered and bruised because of it; and still, he was the one who wiped the blood from the corner of her mouth and sat with her; holding her hand while she cried, vowing that one day he'd make it stop.

The elder brother, Todd, blamed their mother for causing their father to lose his temper and explode into uncontrollable fits of rage, knowing better than to cross the old man's path and believing that everything would be different if only she'd keep her big mouth shut!

Keith grew up to become a respectable member of the community, having opened a medical practice right there in their little town. He also married his college sweetheart and was the proud, doting father of a 4-year-old son and newborn daughter. While Todd on the other hand, barely graduated high school, shacked up with the town whore after knocking her up and made his living working at the local Sunoco station and selling weed to make ends meet.

He is currently serving a life sentence for bludgeoning the town whore to death with a baseball bat; a violent act that occurred when he happened to go home for lunch one afternoon and found her packing her bags in preparation of leaving his sorry ass; a heinous act, witnessed by their 2-year-old son, Joshua; as he stood in the doorway, bottle in one hand, blanket in the other, bundled up and ready to go.

Recognize Me

The night is still and quiet, as the dark cold descends all around. Through the bare trees I wander, making not the faintest sound. For miles you can hear on nights like this, the moon shadows light my way. Across the blanket of snow I go, that softly covers the ground. My heart is forlorn as a mix of emotions stir within me; I am wandering, but I am not lost. A shooting star falls across the sky as if to guide me in the direction where I know you are. I close my eyes and call your name.....

As the single word escapes my lips and is carried off by the wind, I wonder if you would recognize the cool breeze as it brushes your skin and hear the message contained within.

Eternal

Every word was heard
Whether spoken or silent
As the voice of your eyes

Was what I always understood –

Then Blend They

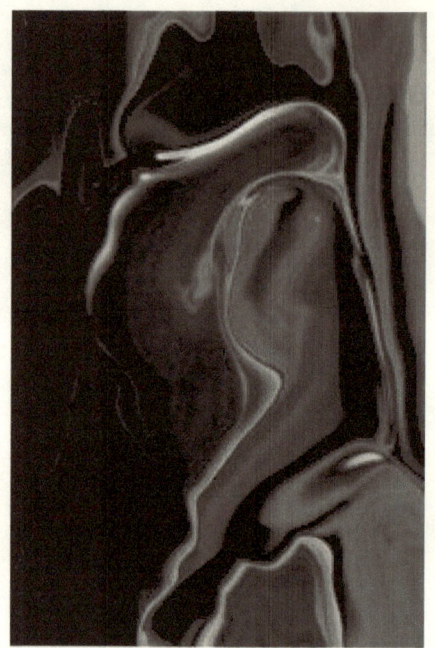

Two paths combine and blend into one
One beautiful and perfect whole
Restless souls mirrored in complexity
Intertwine and mesh in the light

Untamed hearts synchronize in rhythm
Crossing the bounds of time
Emotions sparked, imaginations soared
Each time they came together as one

For a time it was real
Though it felt like a dream
Now they are no more

He showed her how to love
She showed him how to live
That's all either was able to give –

Captured Essence

The words they stir inside my mind, bringing forth release from my pain and sin. Imagination and fantasy effortlessly flow, revealing my soul through stories and verse.

Strangers in silence, who know not of who I am, capturing unknown glimpses on the pages they turn. As they bond with my characters and urge them on, cry at my poetry, as it breaks their heart.

Is there someone out there reading my words…privately delving into my world? Judging…criticizing…abusing my muse, praising my prose as emotions are stirred.

Across sands of time a stranger does linger, in rhythm and rhyme he emerges from nowhere. His music and message I personally relate, as if unlocking the door to my secret self…

You build your world on imagination
You're a decent kind of girl
Your private shelter is isolation
Let your secret place reveal your soul

Drink every drop of life…a reason to fight
Feet on the ground…arms to the sky
Somebody's there to read your words
Somebody's there to see your world –

Phantom Lover

It doesn't matter where
Or what it is I'm doing
When you come to me
Out of nowhere

Random thoughts
Memories
Images locked
Inside my mind

Of the time
We shared
Together

If I close my eyes
Let myself go
I can feel your hands
Upon my flesh
Permanent prints
That can never be
Washed away

Your mind and body
Capture me
Enrapture me
Take me to that place

Where my heart
Smiled
And my soul
Did soar

Momentarily
Peacefully
Greedily

In my mind
On my flesh
Part of you
Remains

And will
Forever
Burn –

We Each Hold the Key

If the power were within us
To travel to worlds outside our own
To learn the secrets that lie beyond the grave
How many of us would make the journey

If the truth of our existence could be found
In the depth of our minds
How deep would we go to find it

What hidden doors
Would we willingly open and walk through
Not knowing what dark shadows
Might lurk on the other side

If we knew for certain
The answers could be found there

The mind knows no limits
The heart has no boundaries
And the soul is capable of soaring
To the endless heights of infinity

The truth exists within all of us
We need only find the key that unlocks the door
And sets it free —

Unconscionable

She got the call just minutes after she arrived late to work; the school guidance counselor, informing her that her daughter had just been rushed to Memorial Hospital, due to what they believed to be a suicide attempt, which occurred in the girl's bathroom, right before first period.

She slammed the phone down, "Mother FUCK…why does this shit always happen to me?!" she yelled and kicked her cubicle wall, while those around her ignored the outburst and kept right on working. She dug out her cell phone, called the boyfriend (of 4 weeks) then whined and begged incessantly, until he agreed to leave work and meet her there. She then called the dad, as she made her way across the parking lot toward her car, realizing suddenly that he'd get to see her new beau, and she hoped like hell it made him jealous!

Row of White Trees

I walked among them in my youth, aware of their presence, but oblivious to their beauty; as I searched for freedom from the bonds I believed restrained me; totally unaware of the inspiration that surrounded me, but completely consumed with finding a way out.

Their fine layers of bark I could easily peel, to pen my plea and send into the world, but what would I say, and who would listen; if I found the words and courage, to express my innermost feelings?

Oh, the ignorance of youth…

Looking Back

He was college-educated with several sheepskins proudly displayed on his office walls, and it was clear that he just didn't get, how someone like me, could write, publish and sell books.

I remember the first time he tested me, though I gave him no reason, I suppose he was just curious. I like words and I like books...I like reading them and writing them. I like using words to form my thoughts and putting them to paper, I explained; but surely you must have had some type of formal education in writing or literature, to be able to create like you do.

"Um...no, I don't write because it's what I want to be, I write because it's who I am." He looked at me strangely, as if I were speaking a foreign language and walked away.

He came to me a week later, having read his sons literary requirement, so as to better help him with the assignment, and he said to me, "I couldn't help thinking, the entire time I was reading, that it was from a woman's voice that the story was written."

The assignment: Mary Shelley's Frankenstein. I just shook my head and thought to myself, *what an asshole!*

Transition

Haunted by memories
Visions…
Images…
Plague the mind
Too many minds
Loss greater than death
Dying a thousand times
Each time I think of you
And remember –

Happy Anniversary

In moments of quiet contemplation when my world is at peace
Or frantic frustration when chaos rules
In times of uncertainly when my vision's askew
Or with eyes wide open and clear is the view

You are my rock…
The foundation on which my world is built

When I find myself lost in this mixed up world
Searching desperately to find my way home
I will follow the road I find lined with love
As this is the one that leads me to you –

Autumn's Splendor

I know that it's fall. Not because I can look out my window and see the changing of the trees. Not because the wind blows cool, upon my suntanned flesh. Not because I shed my summer frocks, wrapping myself in laden clothes. Not because the fire is now lit, for the warmth its flame emits.

I know that it's fall because I can feel it in my soul, and each time I miss it, I feel I'm being cheated. For outside my window my plants do still grow, flowers bursting with colorful blooms, windows down in every room, frigid air keeping me cool.

My heart aches for the beauty of the fall; the last big hurrah before winter's chilly dawn, covers the earth with a blanket of frost. The eternal beauty of autumn's colors lost-

Overwhelming

This passion that I have for you
Is more powerful
Than any feeling I've ever known

It is invisible…

It cannot be seen or measured
But has the power to change me
In an instant

It gives me more joy
Than any mere possession
Ever could

It is the dream of seeing you
Holding you in my arms
Whispering sweet words
Feeling your touch

It lives in my heart
And can be taken by no one
It is mine
It is ours

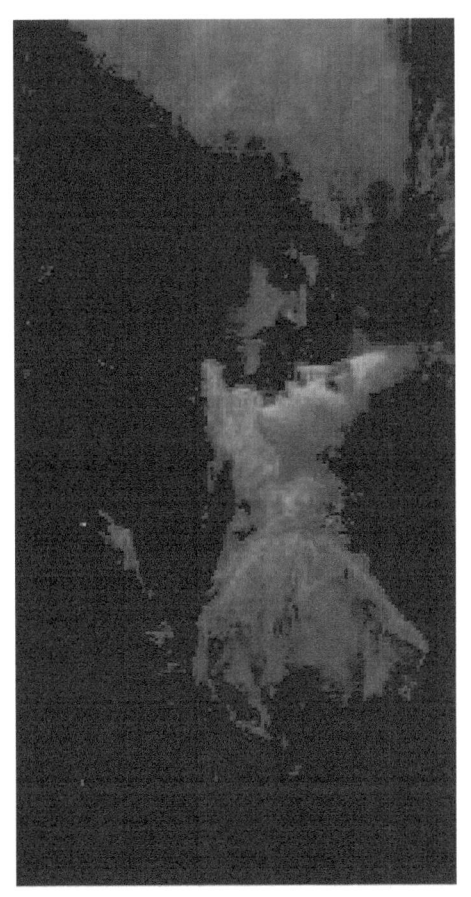

Amour

Who is this person that I've become...

The reflection is the same when I look in the mirror
Yet something about me has changed

I'm no longer the person I'm perceived to be
Since you touched that place inside of me
Rekindling my passion for lust and life
Making my world alive and bright

Your words they touch me, my spirit does soar
It was you who found the key and unlocked the door
The door to my heart the key to our past
We journey unknown through a pleasant repass

How far you will go I wait eagerly to see
You restrain the feelings you have for me
You are not mine, nor am I yours
Unquestionable desire, unfettered amour-

Quote of the day

"Some of us stay forever ourselves, not knowing how to be anything but; hoping to find someone who requires nothing else of us."

No Spoken Words

Many things
I would like to say
All will be spoken in time
Without words –

The Season of You

I watched you many times restless, much more so in the fall, you gaze outside the window, as if hearing a silent call. Something in your nature, sparks this time of year; a vibe you unknowingly emit, draws me ever so near.

I've seen the same in many, some say it's the call of the wild; on you it seems more striking, seductively tempting somehow. I watch you by the fire, flames dancing in your eyes; you look at me and this I see, burning desire that makes me weak.

The things that now I'm thinking, I'd like to do with you; I understand this call of the wild. Oh, to tame the beast in you –

Who Was Scary in your Neighborhood?

She loved when her mom finished off a carton of soda. That meant she got to take the bottles back to the store, cash them in and head a little further up Main Street to the Five and Dime, for a brown sack of penny candy or press-on fingernails. But it wasn't the treats that she got to buy with the bottle money that excited her, so much as being able to browse alone in the store and make mental lists of all the things she wanted.

They lived in the big white house on the corner at the time, only a block from Main Street and the grocery store. Halfway up the block on the left was a doctor's office that sat next to the stone building where the Rainbow Girls gathered. She never knew what they did or who they were, but she knew they were the Rainbow Girls because of the long matching dresses they wore with coordinating hair bows, each a different color of the rainbow. They were beautiful and she always dreamed of being one.

The parking lots of these two buildings connected in the back and merged with the grocery store lot. This day, as she did on most, she took the shortcut and entered the store from the rear entrance by the little loading dock. A wooden ramp led up to the door and you had to walk through a small storage area to get into the store. She didn't think people were actually supposed to use this as an entrance, but she always did and no one ever told her different.

Once inside, she walked along the back of the store, past the meat department on her right and then up the last isle to the register at the front. She wasn't allowed to go to the Five and Dime on this trip, because she had to buy more Pepsi, but her mother had given her money for that, which meant she still got to keep the bottle money for herself. So, she cashed in the bottles then browsed the isles for a few minutes, looking for something she might buy instead of penny candy, before she made her way to the soda isle for her 'must get' purchase. She hated trips when she had to bring home Pepsi, because the carton of full bottles was so heavy and it seemed like it took her forever to make the trek home, as she had to stop and switch hands when the cardboard handle threatened to cut off her fingers. But it was a small price to pay for the privilege of her own spending money.

As she wandered the isles she suddenly had the eerie sensation that someone was watching her, but whenever she turned and looked back there was no one there. As she reached the soda isle, still feeling like she was being followed, she looked up at the big round mirror that hung high in the corner and saw a man peek around the corner, look in her direction then quickly jump back. Her little heart lurched in her chest then started beating double-time, as she grabbed a carton of Pepsi off the shelf and raced to the front of the store. By the time she got back up front to the register, he was already there; Norman Bates; standing, staring, unmoving, in all his creepiness. In hindsight she should have said something to the cashier, but of course she didn't. After all, that was back in the day when it was safe to spend the day outside, running carefree exploring the neighborhood and she was on a mission and just wanted to get home, quick!

She left the store the same way she entered, because her GG used to say that you always leave the same way you enter or its bad luck, and thankfully he was nowhere to be seen. She didn't doodle around on her way home, but kept looking behind her to make sure he wasn't there. She raced up the driveway between the doctor's office and the Rainbow Girls headquarters and safely reached the sidewalk and felt relief wash over here. Until she stopped to transfer the carton to her other hand and looked up ahead and saw Norman standing by a tree; a tree that she had to pass in order to reach home base! She knew she wasn't supposed to, but this was an emergency situation, so she grabbed the soda's up in her arms, looked both ways then quickly crossed the street. He stood unmoving, but she felt his eyes on her nonetheless. She passed him on the opposite side of the street, quickened her pace and looked back to see him crossing to her side of the street. She started to run then, crossed the street one more time and he followed. It was a struggle to run with the carton of soda and she thought surely the bottles would break; the way they were banging against each other, but she never once thought about putting them down.

By the time she got to her corner she was screaming for her mom. Wherever she was in that big old house, her mother heard the screaming and came running out onto the front porch. When she saw her there, her mother was the most beautiful and comforting sight she'd ever seen and she knew she was safe. They quickly went inside, closing and locking the door behind them, as Norman crossed the street then stood on the sidewalk outside their house and looked in. They watched through the sheer curtains, as he just stood there staring at the house, then suddenly he started to walk away. They thought he was gone and made their way through the house to the kitchen, her mother asking a million questions on the way. When they got there her mother looked out the window to see how far up the street he was, but instead she saw Norman in the backyard, standing by the swing-set looking toward the house. That's when her mother called the police.

They came right away and she was disappointed that they didn't have their lights flashing or sirens on, nor did they handcuff Norman and take him away; locking him up in a far away place where she never had to see or fear him again. They just talked to him, right there in the back yard and then a few minutes later, waited and watched while he walked away and disappeared down the street.

Norman was mentally challenged. He lived in the country on the outskirts of town, in an old farmhouse atop a hill with his mother. He liked to walk; that's what he did…every day. He got up, got dressed, had breakfast and then set out walking. Sometimes he'd wander the country roads alone and other times he came into town. This day he was in town and saw a little girl that sparked his interest. He followed her through the store to see what she was doing then followed her home to see where she lived. He thought he might ask her to play once she got there. That little girl was me and Norman was the scariest person in my neighborhood.

Of Human Connections

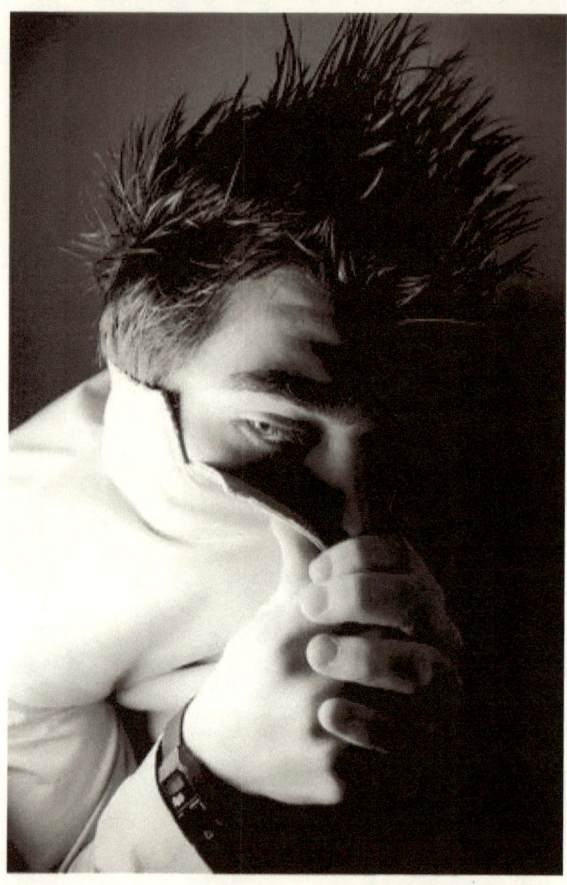

He was
The sum of
All fear

And for a
Moment
I loved him
Madly

Did you feel it?

I know you did. I felt it too. That moment when our eyes met, the attraction was still the same. Everything was there that time had not changed.

You and I alone at last, the clock was ticking the moments quickly passed; but it didn't matter. I was in the presence of you; and for those few hours time stood still for me; the world was silent, centered only on you.

I can still close my eyes and feel you, I don't even have to try; your kiss on my lips, your hand in mine. Those memories of you, how they linger in my mind, to me are the most precious jewels of my life-

Wavering Waters

Feel myself falling
Like a river to the sea
You wash over me completely
Then receded without warning
Leaving not so much
As a ripple in your wake

Breathless

Beautiful you are
with your spirit so high

You came in my life
when I needed a friend

From out of the shadows
you blew in like the wind

And have since taken
my breath away

What More I Want

I do not live alone, yet sometimes I feel so lonely. I do not lack for love, but sometimes it doesn't suit me. I have more than many of this I know, but in my mind I want so much more. To know what it's like to wake by your side, fall asleep each night, your body pressed to mine. To have you hold me as I lay in your arms, not a care in the world; simply lost in your warmth. To reach out and touch you whenever I please, would be such a dream come true for me. None of these things are you able to give, I'll hold tight to my dreams, lock them safely within. Keep making the wishes that can't come true, what more I want is to be with you-

Ezra

With your poise and worldly charm, you took me in your arms, gently brushed the hair from my face. With style and grace it was written on your face, I succumbed to your mysterious ways. "Jilly," you said, as you led me to bed, "I am so enjoying you already," and when I swooned in the darkness of that room, you knew you had me hooked. The first time it happened I couldn't sleep for days, you were always on my mind. The second time it happened I felt I would burst, in the aftermath of carnal bliss, the nights we toyed and taunted, all leading up to this. The next time it happened you took me by surprise, when you casually introduced me to your wife. And in that moment as you strutted in pride, I wished more than anything I was holding a knife-

If Only

If I could be anyone in the world
Anyone at all…

I'd be me
Only I'd be yours —

All I Ask

For a moment let me be
The one who tells you stories
Let me be the one
You lay beside and rest with
Just lay down beside me
If only for a moment –

Wicked Games

He read my words and believed he'd glimpsed inside my soul; as if every character, I played a part; but the only thing he saw, was exactly what I wanted him to see. He thought he was seducing me, when in actuality I was the one doing the seducing. I told him stories and he was content to lay and listen, as my words filled his head and touched his heart; until there was nothing left to say and all was understood. It was then I wrapped myself around his soul; as I took him inside, in the darkness of that room.

Haunting Silence

My words like silent raindrops fall, echoing in the stillness of your silence.

The cold, dark, haunting disquiet that reverberates throughout my entire being, making me want to scream...why...Why...WHY! Until my voice falters, my heart grows heavy, my mind weak; from endless, pointless, painstaking hours, trying to unravel the mystery that is you and fervently searching for a way to bring you back to me, if only for a moment more.

Perfect Stranger

His face is the same, though every time he looks at her, she sees something in his eyes has changed. He carries himself with less dignity; his stride no longer filled with purpose and drive. His smile replaced with a grimace, the unhappiness he's unable to hide.

He is weak and tired, having been beaten and bruised; his pain showing clearly, as if a garment that has already been laid out for him; one he is forced to wear, although it doesn't suit him.

She looks at him and wonders to herself; who is this man, this perfect stranger…this empty shell of the man she knew and loved so well. Where has the warrior gone with his strength and spirit that shown brighter than any star in the sky.

If the visions she sees and the truth they do tell, he will return with a vengeance; wielding courage and confidence that comes from the heart, as a spirit so strong will not be broken for long.

"Where have you been," she asks with a smile. "I never left," he answers simply. "I was just waiting till the time was right to show myself again."

Somewhere in Time

Oh, where is this man
Who torments my body
And haunts my mind
Only so far to be seen
In the depths of my dreams

In search of him now
I must go

But to this place
Where I rest my head
I go with the promise
That he will return to me
Show himself
And love me
Throughout this night

For only in that place
The deepest most secret regions
Of my mind
Does my yearning for him
Surpass all time-

Journal Entry

Writing Prompt: Imagine you're riding the subway in New York City. Next to you is a woman writing in her journal. You notice that she's crying. Feeling nosy, you look to see what she's written and read this: "I fear someone will discover the body soon." Despite the risk, you keep reading. How does the journal entry begin and end?

*****

I told him straight out, it was time for him to go, but did he listen...NO! If only he'd have gotten help in the beginning, perhaps it wouldn't have led to this. What fools!

ME, for thinking I could change him and HIM, for refusing to admit that he had a problem. And sneaking behind my back...as if I couldn't tell the minute I looked in his eyes or he opened his mouth...HA! I should've known what he was doing when he kept going to the hall closet and rummaging around. Looking for his wallet, my ASS! I can't believe he brought the shit back in the house and hid it in the coat pockets. What a loser...pitiful, pathetic loser!

I'd have been better off leaving him right where I found him, instead of thinking I could clean him up and pass him off as husband material, but no....all my friends were married and having babies and I had the fool notion that I wanted to be married too. What a stupid mistake that was! I should've listened to my mother, or better still, the little voice in my head that told me to turn and walk out as I prepared to walk down the isle. But the church was packed and I was a coward. Now I'm a killer.

My only fear is that someone will discover the body soon, before I have a chance to get out of town, but the subway is nearly empty this time of night and not making many stops. I should be able to get a bus ticket to Connecticut without any trouble, and as soon as we leave the city, I'll be home free. My parents will be thrilled when I tell them that I've finally decided to leave for good.

I can't believe I actually did it. What was I thinking? I should've just packed my bags and left when he refused to go, but I didn't. I let my anger turn to rage and when I walked in the bedroom and heard the sound of his breathing…I don't know…something inside just snapped. It really did look like an accident though, the way he fell to the floor and I dropped the lamp beside him.

He was drunk and stumbling out of bed, tripped on the blanket and fell. When he reached for the nightstand to steady himself, he toppled the table and the big ugly lamp with its heavy marble base, fell over and landed on his temple, killing him instantly. No one would ever question whether or not a lamp that size could kill someone if it were to land in just the right spot. I'm so glad my aim was dead on (no pun intended), as I'd have hated to have to hit him more than once.

I feel prying eyes from the stranger sitting in the seat behind me, who I think just tried to look over my shoulder. Besides, the tears are coming again and I can hardly see to write. They aren't tears of regret they're tears of joy…that I'm finally free! Will write more later; when I get to mom and dads.

Ask Alice

Like Alice through the looking glass
The things I saw weren't really there
The words you spoke were backwards truths
You never knew the way I felt

Your words of want sustained me
Made me feel alive
Touching some place inside of me
I believed had long since died

The mind plays a wicked game
When lead solely by the heart
Once I found you in my life again
I wanted to believe we never would part

To have a little piece of you
Any way I could
My days became much brighter
Less lonely were the nights

Like a dirty puddle on the floor
My heart to you I eagerly poured
The contentment I found within my soul
The truth of you crept in and stole

Maudlin prose of a lonely heart
Grasping for that long-lost ghost
The one that foretells my future
Continually haunts my past
Time has a way of changing things
No matter how good
They never seem to last

Alone you've left me stumbling in the dark
Was it the words I gave you from my heart
How could something that felt so real
Turn out to be an illusion surreal

You make me wonder who you are
And what it is you're thinking
Down the rabbit hole searching I go
Looking for Alice; maybe she knows-

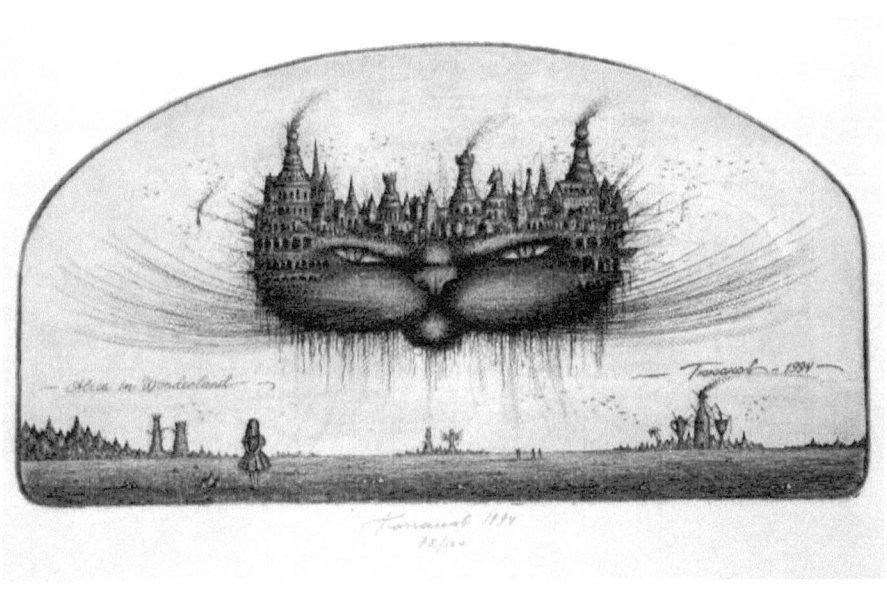

Ray of Light

On a dark lonely night you appeared
Erasing the things I secretly feared

You touched a place inside of me
Which no one has before
The night you chose to enter
As I held open the door

Deep inside I felt the light
That lit my life was growing dim
With your words you touched my heart
Made it bright again

And so now if you went away
The darkness would abound
And in a sea of sadness
Slowly I would drown-

Tired of being sorry

Sometimes, usually in the morning, when everyone has gone and he is left alone, I feel his thoughts turn and touch me like a secret caress, and in that moment I feel his truth…his longing…for that mystery he found, beyond the silver moon.

Parting Thoughts

Alone in the dark I lay in this loft
Just minutes away from where you are
I close my eyes, whisper your name
And wonder if somehow you hear me

Would you come to me if you could…

Do you still feel my kiss on your lips
As I feel yours on mine
The days pass quickly
Slip through my hands
Already I'm out of time

And I wonder if ever I'll see you again

Was it just a stolen moment as I passed through
The last thing I want is to leave
When I've come so far and only just found you

I've never known anyone like you
No one comes close, no one ever will
Do you understand what I'm feeling now
Does is make a difference in your life somehow

I look at you, it makes me want to cry
Those blue-gray eyes that change
With the color of your passion

Every part of me comes alive when I'm with you
I'd stay here forever to be where you are

I'd take down my hair for you
I'd sit home and wait for you
Anything you want me to do

If only I could…

But as I sit here listening to the rain in the trees
Just hours away from leaving
I can't help but wonder where you are
And what it is you're thinking

Are you tormented with guilt as would be your nature
Or is there a part of you that wants me still
I have touched you and tasted the passion of your kiss
In my mind that memory will always live

I'll be here always waiting, hoping for the day
Another stolen moment to come our way
It was always only you…and always will be-

A Day on the St. Johns

Eyes closed, face raised toward the sun as it warms from the inside out.
Carefree and unburdened, gliding gently across the water, lost in this day
so long in coming. Troubles left tied at the dock as the current leads to a
world that renews hope, lifts spirits and soothes the soul;
Effortlessly…peacefully…naturally-

Ghost Whispers

Twenty years have gone by and still he comes to see her from time to time. His visits leave her with a foreboding feeling that lasts for days, sometimes weeks after. But foreboding was a feeling that she'd always associated with him. Theirs was a spiritual union, although tumultuous at times, their lives meshed and what they shared was nothing less than magical.

During his visits they converse freely and he offers words of wisdom or comfort, as most often something is troubling her; something she may not be consciously aware of, until he broaches the subject and forces her to step back and take a deeper look at what's going on in her world. Somehow he always knows. Occasionally he reaches out and touches her and although such moments are fleeting, the sensation lingers long after he has gone.

It's during those times when her mind and body are at total peace and the door to alternate worlds lay wide open that she is most receptive to his visits. Dreams, as they are simply the remembrance of what the spirit has seen in sleep, constituting actual spirit-to-spirit meetings; something she had longed for in her youth, but was reluctant to accept as reality later in life.

But why the reluctance…

For the moment their lips first touched, she experienced her first vision, or premonition, if you will; as her body stirred with emotions and sensations that she'd never before experienced. She felt as though she could simply wish herself away and let the feeling of pure and utter bliss whisk her into eternity. Instead, she saw a brilliant light flash inside her mind, followed by an image that shook her to the core of her soul, and she knew in that instant, that not only was their time together limited, but that his death was imminent.

For two years she carried the fear close to her heart, yet she never said anything to him or anyone else about what she'd seen. Instead, she diligently prayed for his safety every time they separated and she made the most of each moment they shared. Yet somehow, even though she gave herself completely, to him and to prayer, she often felt it wasn't enough.

Twenty years later he still visits; bringing messages of comfort and hope. Comfort in the fact that after all this time he has not forgotten and her prayers were not in vain. Hope in the knowledge that life is not over once we leave the bonds of our earthly bodies, as he did on that fateful night twenty years ago.

His message is clear and unwavering in its certainty. We are not human beings who on occasion have a spiritual experience in this world…we are spiritual beings experiencing a temporary human existence. The veil separating our worlds is thin and can be crossed at will, if ones belief and desire are great enough to withstand the journey.

The Journey

As nightfall descends, she leaves the bank of propriety, on a quest to forbidden shores, ignoring the flames as they dance in the breeze and extinguish one by one. A free spirit and old soul, listening to the voice of her heart; guided by the light of desperation and desire that will lead her to the place where her twin soul awaits.

Separated by distance and time, she wonders if he still holds memories of the magic created, when their hearts and minds were synchronized to a rhythm all their own. Not a flight-of-fancy, found in fairy tales and superstition, but a result of their combined energy that existed at all times and could be harnessed and used at will.

Endless hours spent. Discussing ideals, dreams and plans for a future that centered on the virtue of worth, advantage and beneficial qualities of creativity, in relation to being true to oneself. She cannot help but wonder if he still holds strong, or the person she came to know so well, simply no longer exists.

For not unlike a warrior in battle, forced to distance himself from the realities of his actions in order to forge ahead and complete the tasks that must be done; he gathers memories and remnants, locking them away in a place so far from the surface of his true self that the threat of them being lost forever is despairing, yet necessary for his survival.

In moments of silence when he's alone inside his mind, does he feel her spirit lingering and the enduring longing to hold it within his grasp? Still lucky, does he feel, to have been taken into her private world; to be guided by her light, to have felt the warmth of the fire that burns within her soul and the emotional comfort that her soft caress and touch did bring?

Or has the truth of her that he knew so well, been tainted by time, regret and lies? Was the deceit and betrayal, more than his soul could bear? Has he cast aside all they shared, vowing to never again let the thought of her enter his mind? Submitting to the pretense of what time has created, though self-confessed, is not enough to sustain him.

And if during her quest, an untimely demise is met, would he cast aside all doubt and feel pain for the loss? Would he remember her with a smile, as he sits alone, along the rocky shore of life, close his eyes and picture her there? Remembering her words and the truth they held; in his moments of quiet revelation, accept the profoundness of their experience and reemerge with a changed preconceived notion of reality and of himself.

Only time will tell the answers she seeks, in the journey that lies ahead.

And a Child Shall Lead Them

When we hear the word "Witch" most of us automatically think of the Salem Witch Trials that took place in the late 1600's, in Salem Massachusetts. The truth is, witch hunts began as early as the 12th century and ideas about witches can be found in most cultures around the world. Most beliefs are based on the idea of people possessing the ability to harm by the use of spiritual forces.

According to witch trial judges, there are two specific parts to the witchcraft crime. The first was practicing evil magic against other people and the second was the witch having a direct connection or pact with the Devil. Legal systems were formed by professional people who dedicated their lives to the persecution of women they believed were a threat to society, thus condemning them as witches. Some scholars suggest that Christian ideology, imposed on ordinary people to believe in male supremacy was the reasoning behind the oppression and persecution of women.

Although methods of torture and execution varied widely throughout various countries, it's safe to say that those acting on the authority of God, showed no mercy to the accused. These methods included sleep depravation, "the strappado," which was a pulley that raised the accused off the ground by their arms or legs and "the rack," an instrument of compression that consisted of head clamps, leg clamps and thumb clamps. Occasionally, witch chairs were used, which were heated by fire from below as the witch was strapped to it. In 1591 Scotland the most severe and cruel pain in the world was reported to have been inflicted on one accused witch, referred to as "the bootes." During this procedure, the witch's legs were crushed and beaten together as small as possible until the bones and flesh were so bruised that blood and marrow spewed forth in great abundance. Regardless of which form was used, once the torture was complete the witch could then expect to be burned alive at the stake or hanged on the gallows.

All forms of torture and execution were inflicted with the blessings of the church, as the eradication of witches represented victory for the supreme power of God.

The following story is my fictional interpretation, based on factual evidence I have read regarding the witch trials of Salem. Excerpts from the book, "Memorable Providences, Relating to Witchcraft and Possessions" by Cotton Mather, are taken from published text as presented by the author. Names, dates and any detailed accounts of the accused and executed are accurate.

*****

And a Child Shall Lead Them

Betty Parris and her cousin, Abigail Williams, were just 5 and 7 years old when they first heard the tales of the scandal that rocked the little village of Salem. Witchcraft, possession, devils and molestation; the words alone were titillating and conjured thoughts and feelings otherwise forbidden and unknown to their young hearts and minds. Yet it was all anyone could speak or think of. Even in their hometown of Boston, the stories brought a level of excitement and scandal, the likes of which their community had never known. But once Goody Glover, the evil witch, was hanged, the excitement died down and all was calm.

The Parris's were a well-to-do family with connections to some of the most distinguished families in Boston. Their wealth was due to Samuel Parris' marriage to Elizabeth Eldridge and the land in Barbados that Samuel had inherited from his father; his father having passed away while Samuel was studying at Harvard.

Samuel was a successful Boston merchant, who supported his family in a manner that left them wanting for nothing. But for Samuel, the position was unfulfilling and left him with an ever increasing desire to change his vocation. He began by filling in for absent ministers at informal church gatherings, which led to negotiations with the village of Salem to become the new preacher. He eventually packed up his family, much to their dismay and they came to settle in the village of Salem in 1689. It was then that his full time ministry began.

There immediately began talk among the congregation about the family's wealth and the rumors that had started in Boston, regarding the Parris' live in slave-girl, Tituba. Some said that not only did she oversee the day-to-day household duties, but in the years before Samuel married Elizabeth, that she had acted as his concubine as well.

It was a disgrace, they said, for a minister of God to allow such an evil woman to care for his family. She was evil because she refused to succumb to their Puritanical ways and held strong to her own beliefs and customs. Something that Samuel had never given a thought to, since receiving her as payment for a debt by one of his business associates in Barbados, when she was just 15 years of age.

Tituba was an Indian woman, originally from an Arawak village in South America, where she was captured as a child, taken to Barbados as a captive, and sold into slavery. Her story was heart-wrenching and Samuel would no more consider forcing her to submit to his Christian ways, as he would consider practicing hers. Her heritage and customs were all that she had left of the life she knew as a child and Samuel was not about to take that away from her, regardless of what anyone said.

Unfortunately, the villagers didn't agree and made life difficult for the Parris family. Although Reverend Parris and his wife, Elizabeth, were able to turn the other cheek, the children, however, were picked on and taunted regularly; and soon they came to hate their new home in Salem; Abigail and Betty especially, as the other girls could be absolutely wicked in their taunting.

As rumors and speculation continued to spread, dissatisfaction with the new minister began to spread as well, and the congregation vowed to drive him out. A committee was formed and it was agreed that not only would they not impose a tax to support his salary, but they refused to supply firewood for the family to use throughout the cold New England winter.

In response, Reverend Parris's sermons began to focus on warnings of Satan descending upon Salem, taking hold of the villagers and congregation, thus causing them to turn on him and his family. This did not produce the results he had anticipated; in fact, it seemed to add fuel to the fire, as things from there got progressively worse.

*****

The subject of Tituba had never failed to stir interesting conversation with the other Bostonian children, and Abigail and Betty often took every opportunity to tout their knowledge of fortune telling and other non-Christian activities that they had learned from her. But this was not Boston and Abigail and Betty were growing desperate to gain the acceptance of their peers.

They thought about running away, but that would only be a temporary solution to their ever-growing problem, as they were certain to be found and then punished accordingly. No, they agreed that they had to do something drastic, but between the two of them, they could come up with nothing. That was, until that fateful day when they found the book.

"Memorable Providences, Relating to Witchcraft and Possessions," written by the former Minister of Salem, Cotton Mather, gracing the shelves in the meager Parris library.

Abigail now 11 and Betty 9 snatched the book from its resting place, on a cold winter day in the year of our Lord, 1691 and proceeded to devour its contents, in the privacy of the upstairs room in which Abigail and Betty shared.

Since the book was only one, they decided to take turns reading aloud in hushed tones to each other, lest they be caught and punished. As Abigail read through the mundane introduction, she silently wished to herself that she had allowed Betty to go first, as requested, but as she came to the end, she found a renewed excitement in Cotton Mather's words, as she spoke them in a tone mocking his own.

"But I can with contentment beyond mere patience, give those rescinded sheets unto the Stationer, when I see what pains Mr. Baxtrer, Mr. Glanvil, Dr. More and several other great names have taken to publish histories of witchcrafts and possessions onto the world. I said let me also run after them; and this with the more alacrity because I have tidings ready. Go then, my little book, as a lackey, to the more elaborate essays of those learned men. Go tell mankind that there are Devils and Witches; and that though those night-birds least appear where the daylight of the gospel comes, yet New England has had examples of their existence and operation; and that not only the wigwams of Indians, where the Pagan Pow Wows often raise their masters in the shapes of bears and snakes and fires, but the house of Christians where our God has had his constant worship, have undergone the annoyance of evil spirits."

"Go tell the world what prayers can do beyond all Devils and Witches and what it is that these monsters love to do; and through the Demons in the audience of several standers-by threatened much disgrace to thy author, if he let thee come abroad, yet venture that and in this way seek in just revenge on them for the disturbance they have given to such as have called on the name of God."

The girls continued reading the tale, which described in great detail, the misfortune that had befallen the Goodwin family and four of their children, at the stupendous hand of witchcraft. The four children, who had enjoyed a religious education and possessed observable affection for Divine and sacred things, were afflicted with unaccountable stabs and pains, odd fits, bodily distortions and bouts that left them deaf, dumb and sometimes blind, and absolutely amazed their spectators.

Some weeks prior, the eldest Goodwin daughter had accused their laundress, the daughter of an ignorant and scandalous woman, of stealing some of their missing linen. The laundress' mother cursed at the girl, upon her daughter's defense and not long after, the attacks against the Goodwin girl began. Then one by one, the other three children came to suffer the same torture at the hands of this witch, who was then trapped and brought to trial. Unfortunately, the attacks didn't stop once the witch was hanged, thus lending proof of her supernatural power that she wielded from the grave.

Betty and Abigail remembered it well, even though they were only 5 and 7 and living in Boston at the time. The air buzzed with activity in the days between the witches arraignment and condemnation, as it was the single most dramatic thing to have happened in New England. The hype was intoxicating and everyone seemed to be in a constant state of hyperactivity, turmoil and frenzy.

As they continued to read one passage after another, their own excitement grew, as the melodrama contained in Cotton Mather's book was spine-tingling and inspiring, and before they had even reached the end, they were formulating their own plan.

*****

Two days later, Betty began developing strange symptoms, as if some unseen force were pinching, pricking and choking her. Reverend Parris contacted the local doctor, who unfortunately was unable to diagnose the problem. Several more physicians were called in, and it wasn't until Betty was examined by Dr. William Griggs, that the suggestion of witchcraft was first voiced. The Reverend immediately organized prayer meetings and days of fasting in an attempt to rid Betty of her symptoms and the evil force that possessed his daughter. In the days that followed, his niece, Abigail, became afflicted with the same symptoms that Betty suffered, followed days later by an attack on Ann Putnam and soon other village girls as well.

In the privacy of their room, in times of pause from the forces of evil that tormented and tortured them, Betty and Abigail celebrated in secret. Not only had they managed to gain the attention and sympathy of the entire village, but they now had the support and friendship of other girls in the village, that at one time had mocked and teased them, but now followed their lead and had become afflicted as well.

Although her actions would eventually lead to accusations of witchcraft, Tituba could not stand by and do nothing with such suffering happening all around her. She decided to prepare a "witch cake," which was a mixture of rye and urine. The cake would be cooked and fed to a dog, in the belief that the dog would then reveal the identity of Betty's afflicter.

The girls were ecstatic when Tituba came to them and said that she wanted to help. Betty readily agreed to participate in her plan, by providing her with a cup full of urine to be added to the witch cake. It was the most exciting thing that had happed to them since moving to Salem, much more exciting than just telling tales to the children in Boston, because now *they* were the focus, not Tituba.

In the mean time, Reverend Parris was doing everything he could to support Betty and the other afflicted girls, including fanning the flames of witchcraft suspicion from his pulpit. Then he got word of the witch cake Tituba had made and in his rage he beat her into confession. Fearing for her very life, Tituba, who had been a faithful servant to her master, confessed to being a witch.

What began as an innocent and childish game had suddenly taken a serious and scary turn that the girls no longer wanted to be part of. Four weeks had passed and now the attention was focused on Betty, as she was the first to become afflicted. She was visited on a regular basis by ministers and townspeople, who interrogated and pressured her to name the person responsible for her behavior and affliction. Unable to take the mental strain and fear caused by her interrogators, Betty saw only one way out and identified Tituba as her afflicter.

Once the word spread, it wasn't long before the other girls were interrogated and following suit, accused Sarah Good, a homeless beggar and social misfit and Sarah Osborne, an old quarrelsome woman who hadn't attended church in over a year. Relieved that the game had finally come to an end, the girls would now share a secret bond that would seal their friendship forever.

That was, until a few days later when arrest warrants were issued for Tituba, Sarah Good and Sarah Osborne. The bond the girls shared quickly became a secret pact, as they vowed to maintain their innocence at whatever cost. They knew they would be forced to testify and convince the entire community that these women were to blame for their afflictions. Should their devious plot ever be found out, they couldn't imagine the severity of the punishment they would be forced to endure.

*****

And so the focus was shifted, from the afflicted to the accused and the girls were called upon to testify to their experiences, in the presence of magistrates, physicians, parishioners and townspeople. As if actresses giving stage performances to a packed house, they were only too happy to play their roles as innocent victims touched by the hand of evil. And the audience played right into their hands.

It wasn't long before they realized that the more elaborate their stories, the more excited the crowd became, cheering and jeering as they told their tales and demonstrated afflictions, as they pretended to be attacked by an invisible force, right before the eyes of the awestruck crowd.

It was exhilarating, intoxicating and seductive, the power that these young girls wielded over grown men and women and the fear they struck into the hearts of the other children. Soon they were accusing anyone who had ever given them a sideways glance or done anything at one time or another to make them mad; and the best part was that everyone believed them, no matter how outrageous their claims.

The intensity in the court grew hour by hour, day by day and soon it wasn't enough to simply attend the hearings and sit idly by and watch the performances play out. Others wanted to be part of the outlandish production and soon many more came forward with claims and accusations, that they too had been the victim of witchcraft.

Between the months of June and September of 1692, total chaos erupted and the foundation that once upheld the community of Salem, was shattered and anyone who scoffed at the accusations put themselves at great risk of becoming targets of accusation.

Hundreds were arrested, tortured and imprisoned on charges of witchcraft, including the 4-year-old daughter of accused witch, Sarah Good. Shackled by heavy chains in a dark, dank prison cell, the child would later watch as her mother was carted off to Gallows Hill, where her life was ended by hanging and her last thoughts were of her precious child imprisoned and facing the same fate. Her child was spared the noose, but remained imprisoned for eight months, where she cried her heart out and slowly went insane.

Eventually the bloodlust began to ebb, thanks to Reverend John Hale, who maintained a level of common sense in the midst of rampant insanity and raised doubts as to how so many respectable people in so small a compass of land could be guilty of having abominably leapt into the lap of the Devil at once. It was then that Reverend Increase Mather, President of Harvard College and father to Cotton Mather, the author of the book that was likely the root cause of the evil and hysteria that had befallen Salem, published a work in which he argued that, "It were better that ten suspected witches should escape than one innocent person should be condemned."

A total of nineteen men and women were hanged at Gallows Hill on charges of witchcraft; one elderly man was slowly crushed to death, under a pile of heavy stones, for refusing to submit to trial, before the hysteria and insanity that swept through Salem came to an end.

All in the name of God.

In the Distance

She could see the clearing in the distance, a glowing light at the end of what seemed to be a never-ending tunnel, but the faster she ran, the farther away the opening seemed.

She wondered for a fleeting moment, if perhaps her mind was playing tricks with her and she should alter her course. Knowing that what lie in the shadows of the forbidden forest, paled in comparison to the horrors that lie just beyond the fencerow, still she dared not stray from the path that lay open before her.

Nor would she give in to the frustration and fear that threatened to slow her pace; even though her limbs ached with fatigue and her breathing was labored. Freedom was close at hand and she refused to look back; as her very life depended on reaching her goal that lay in wait, in the distance up ahead.

Ghost Rider

We were friends, best friends in my estimation, although he was too cool to hang with me at school on a regular basis, he would occasionally sit with me at the burger joint across the street at lunch, if all the other tables were full. But after school, once we'd had dinner and were settled in for the night, my phone would ring like clockwork and it would be him, calling to shoot the shit and make me laugh.

He said he liked the sound of my laugh and the way my face lit up when I smiled, and that he could hear the smile in my voice. I believed him.

My grandfather was self-employed, delivering supplies to local bars, his happened to own one of them on my grandfather's route, and they knew each other well. It was a biker bar and he'd often tell me stories of the people that frequented the place and how one day he was going to ride his Harley cross country and see America; free of worry and responsibility, just enjoying life and taking all it had to offer.

He spoke of Sturgis, the Black Hills of South Dakota and the biker runs held there each year; vowing that he'd be there, just as soon as we were out of school and he had the money to do it. This was his dream and when he spoke to me about it, images were conjured in my mind, of an older, wiser, happier him, fulfilling his dreams and living his destiny.

I beat him to Sturgis, traveling with my parents that summer for 3 weeks. I was sixteen years old and more interested in the romance novel I'd brought along for entertainment than the beauty of the country around me. We'd even talked about asking our parents if he could go along, but it wasn't meant to be.

We were visiting Mount Rushmore, having traveled many, many miles mingled with hundreds of bikers heading to the same destination. It was exhilarating and almost seductive the way they traveled in a pack and hadn't a care in the world. I knew then what fueled his dream, because even though I was stuck in a car with my family, I was living it. I couldn't wait to tell him about it, so I began penning a letter as we rode, gazing out the window as the motorcycles passed us by, pipes roaring so loud that I could feel it in my soul.

He pulled up and parked his Harley right beside us, the giant mountain with carved faces in the distance; the same strawberry-blonde hair shining in the sun, a little longer and windblown. The same faint line of freckles across the bridge of his nose; the same build, only matured into that of a man's; the same blue eyes, the same smile, and undeniable recognition when he looked at me.

I couldn't breathe, as my heart was lodged in my throat and I felt lightheaded. I thought this had to be a hallucination due to the change in altitude or maybe someone slipped something in my coke back at the diner. Whatever it was it scared the hell out of me, because just a few feet away, stood the vision of my friend that I'd conjured in my mind a thousand times as he shared his dreams of the future with me.

We toured the Mount and I wasn't the least bit impressed, but when we drove a little further south and came to the Crazy Horse Monument that got my attention. I stood gazing up at the monstrous site, thinking to myself what a horrible shame and disgrace it was that they'd abandoned the project, and it was then that my fascination, admiration and undying respect for the Native American Culture was born. I was contemplating their plight on the way back to the car, when I happened upon him again. He looked at me and smiled, winked and nodded, as if he'd been reading my mind, understood what I was feeling and agreed with me whole-heartedly.

We left and headed off to our next destination and that was the last time I saw the familiar stranger. We called my grandparents at one of our stops and I grabbed the phone from my mom. I exchanged hellos with grandma and I told her I was ready to come home and then I'll never forget what she said next...

"Honey, your grandpa was delivering supplies this morning and wanted me to ask you if you know a boy named Chris Sellers. He's from Williamsburg and about your age."

"Duh...he's my best friend! His grandpa owns the bar grandpa delivers to." There was a silent pause, during which time my grip tightened on the phone. "Why, grandma, what is it?" I said, not really wanting to know. "I'm sorry honey. He was killed in a jeep accident yesterday," she said matter-of-factly, but with sorrow and regret in her voice. I don't remember if I said anything else, gave the phone back to my mom or what. I just remember the numbness, the all-consuming numbness.

We drove well into the night and I'll never forget the stars that filled the sky that night; more stars than I've ever seen in my life, as if the entire universe was just outside my window. I grieved in silence, as the miles wore on and I gazed to the heavens for answers to all the questions that filled my young mind; knowing in my heart that my friend was gone forever and my life would never be the same. And although I didn't understand how or why, I knew beyond a doubt that somehow, Chris was fulfilling his dream, living his destiny and had shared the most special part of it with me that day.

And that's when my true passion for life, death and all that lies in between began.

W h y

Lonely in the dark of night when no one is around
The beating of my heart the only audible sound
Close my eyes and picture you there
Across from me you sit in that worn leather chair
A smile plays across your face
A knowing look sparks in your eyes
I hang my head in sorrow and ask myself why
Why do I do this a million times a day
Imagine you there in so many different ways-

The Impaler Prince

I am a man with a penchant for killing; whose soul has been damned and corrupted by mere mortals, who knew me not lest for my bloodline and looked upon themselves as mine enemy. I have been driven to the brink of insanity and watched, as if a bystander, while my grasp of reality slowly ebbed away. I have delighted in the carnal pleasures of many a wondrous Maiden, to the point of obsession and beyond. I am cruel, wicked, powerful, feared and revered. I am evil incarnate and no man dare attempt to put an end to my madness, lest he too become an unfortunate himself.

I am Vlad Tepes, son of Vlad Dracul, Prince of Wallachia Romania.

My story begins when I was a mere child, on the edge of my eleventh year. I was enjoying my life, for all intents and purposes, living with my father and elder brother, Mircea, and younger brother Radu, in the Palace of Tirgoviste. As the son of a nobleman, I was naturally trained and educated in the skills of war and peace deemed necessary to become a Christian Knight, as was my lot in life, set forth by my father's position.

Under the cloak of darkness, on a night when the skies were roiling with tempest clouds, my brother Mircea and I were stolen from our palace home, taken as hostages and imprisoned for six long, agonizing years. In the beginning I held to the belief that at any moment, my father and his faithful Knights would appear out of the darkness, as if a light sent from the heavens above, to rescue us from the hell that had befallen us. But they did not come and there was no light to penetrate the darkness of despair that I came to know so well.

Undoubtedly, the horrific, inhumane and unnatural experiences of torture that I was forced to endure during my imprisonment, cast upon me by my father's political adversary, caused me to develop an unparalleled loathing for society as a whole. This living nightmare that I unwillingly suffered, stole my virtue of innocence, befuddled my mind and turned my thoughts to those of revenge and bloodlust; hardening my heart and blackening my soul.

I had stared into the many faces of evil and was forced to submit to its will. But in my darkest hour, I held to the belief that I would one day, unleash my wrath one-hundred fold on my abusers and the Devil himself would beg me for mercy.

*****

I was in my seventeenth year when they came and informed me of my father's assassination and the brutal torture and death of my brother, Mircea. They described to me in great detail the way in which my brother had been beaten, blinded by hot iron stakes that pierced his eyes and then buried alive; all at the hands of the boyars of Tirgoviste.

Upon receiving the news, I was released by my captors and given the support of a force of Turkish cavalrymen and a contingent of troops that were lent to me by Pasha Mustafa Hassan, so that I could act as their own candidate and fulfill their order in seizing the throne of Wallachia. Unfortunately, I was unsuccessful in my seizure and the throne was claimed by none other than Vladislav II, the assassin who organized the deaths of my father and brother.

My failure simply incensed my lust for blood, as I was forced to patiently wait eight long years before receiving satisfaction in the killing of my mortal enemy and seizing my rightful position on the throne. It was then that my true reign began.

I unleashed my pent-up fury through brutal acts of punishment, on all those I deemed worthy of my attentions. My controversial reputation quickly spread throughout the land and soon I would come to be known as, Vlad Tepes Dracula; The Impaler Prince.

Once in a position of power, my philosophies and insistence of honesty and order became know fairly quickly. Almost any crime, from lying and stealing to killing, would result in punishment by impalement. It was my belief that all subjects must work and be productive members within the community and therefore, I looked upon the poor vagrants and beggars of my land, as nothing more than lowly thieves.

Consequently, I invited all the poor and sick of Wallachia to my court, in Tirgoviste, to participate in a great feast. Once all those in attendance had their fill of food and drink, which lasted well into the night, I made a brief appearance and then ordered the hall to be boarded up and set aflame. Needless to say, there were no survivors and my actions cast a shadow of fear and dismay into the hearts of all.

Once the task of ridding the land of all the beggars and thieves was complete, I could then concentrate on my first major act of revenge, which was directed at the boyars of Tirgoviste, for the conspiracy and killing of my father and brother. And so, in celebration of Easter, I invited all the boyars and their families to participate in a princely feast.

During the celebration I participated in verbal exchange with several guests on the topic of how many princes had ruled during their lifetimes. It appeared as if all those in attendance had outlived several princes, although I knew beyond a doubt that such a fate would not befall my reign. It was during this conversation that I ordered all the assembled guests arrested on the spot.

The elder boyars and their families were impaled on stakes and all those who remained were forced to march fifty miles from the capital to the town of Poenari. The trek was quite grueling, but no one was permitted to rest until their destination was reached. At that point, the remaining survivors were enslaved and ordered to build a fortress on the ruins of an old outpost that overlooked the Arges River. Many died during the process, but I was successful in creating a new nobility and obtaining a fortress for future emergencies; a fortress which would come to be known as Castle Dracula.

*****

I became quite well known for my brutal and inhumane punishment techniques, which I had concocted and perfected during the years of my imprisonment. The methods in which I chose my victims to die depended largely on my state of mind and what loathsome memories happen to be haunting me at the time. It was my belief that no torture cast upon my victims could come close in comparison to that which I had withstood and survived. Many believed that I was perversely fascinated with death and thus the reason for my actions. I did not attempt to convince them otherwise, lest it be a waste of my time to try and explain the hatred and loathing contempt that consumed me to the core of my very being.

What I found truly fascinating was that no one took notice of the fact that the killings very rarely happen by my own hand. Thousands of eager gentry as well as paupers, waited anxiously in line to be among my chosen assassins; to do my bidding and quench their own perverse thirst for death and mutilation. This simply proved my theory that all men were evil and deserved to die. Unbeknownst to them, each assassin was placed on my special list of victims that should die the slowest, most agonizing and painful deaths, only to be replaced by the next eager gent at the head of the line. Who would, in time, befall the same fate.

My methods of torture were a clear indication of my sanity or lack thereof, yet they were never questioned and always carried out to my exact specifications. I often ordered people to be skinned alive, boiled in a vat, decapitated, blinded, strangled, hanged, burned, roasted, hacked, nailed, buried alive or stabbed to death. As one can well imagine, the mere listing of my methods exhausts me; however, tis necessary in order for one to comprehend the depth of my madness and despair.

On occasion, immediate death was spared the victim. Those so chosen were forced to endure their remaining hours or days with their ears, noses, sexual organs or limbs cut off. However, beyond a doubt and by far the most gruesome way of dying imaginable, was by impalement on the stake.

Impalement techniques varied, but most often a horse was attached to each of the victim's legs and a sharpened stake was gradually forced into the buttocks until it emerged through the victim's mouth. It was necessary to oil the end of the stake and great care was taken so that the stake was not too sharp, lest the victim might die too quickly due to sudden shock. Death by impalement should be slow and painful and if done properly, the victim could endure for hours or sometimes days thereafter.

*****

Since it was my belief that all of mankind was corrupt and evil, no one was immune to my attentions. My victims included women and children, great lords and peasants, ambassadors of foreign lands and merchants. Many attempted to justify my actions on the basis of political necessity, even though the death count under my reign reached ten, twenty and even thirty-thousand killings at one time. Yes, thirty-thousand in one fell swoop. Unbelievable is it not…

This particular incident, which I do tend to be boastful of, took place on St. Bartholomew's Day, in the year 1459. I gave the order that thirty-thousand merchants and boyars of Transylvania should be impaled. In an attempt to better appreciate the results of my orders, I commanded that my table be set up among the forest of stakes that held their grisly impaled victims, many of which were still alive.

While a nearby executioner diligently hacked apart another victim, I invited my faithful boyars to join me in a feast of celebration. While dining, I couldn't help but notice one of my boyars holding his nose in an effort to alleviate the terrible stench of clotting blood and emptied bowels that not only surrounded our table, but undoubtedly could be detected for miles away. I asked if he found the stench oppressive and his dishonest response was that his only concern was for my personal health and welfare. In a moment of humorous irony, I immediately ordered him impaled on the spot; on a stake higher than all others, so that he might enjoy the last moments of his life above the offending odors.

There was never a pause between my orders being voiced and carried out; and in that moment, literally surrounded by a sea of death and destruction as far as the eye could see, I realized that no man were brave enough to stop my insanity. The political situation surrounding my land had little or nothing to do with my reign of terror, nor were they a result of my attempt at enforcing my own moral code upon the land. My actions were purely self-centered in nature and an ill-fated attempt to release the demons that plagued and haunted my tortured soul.

I would, however, not come to know such a release, until the moment of my own death in December of the year 1476. After my death, my body was decapitated by the Turks and my head was sent to Constantinople where the Sultans proudly and befittingly displayed it on a stake, as proof of my death.

Let my reign of terror be a lesson to those who believe themselves beyond reproach, and willingly corrupt the hearts, minds and bodies of others, due to their own lack of humanity and sickness of soul. Nothing was gained me, by the tens of thousands of deaths that occurred by my order. My soul that once was pure and corrupted at the hand of man, is now damned for all eternity, by an entity who wields such atrocities that my mortal heart and mind could never have fathomed.

Evil begets evil and no good can surely come of it, yet goodness shall reign in the hearts of those who cast it aside and in their darkest hour of despair and suffering, seek the Truth, the Light and the Way.

Beyond the Invisible

She had the eyes of a searcher, the eyes of a dreamer, and in those
glorious moments when she connected with herself, the eyes of a seer.
Wandering; sometimes lost, sometimes because there was no other
choice; guided by spirit in all her hunger and desire; on a quest to
discover that lost part of her self and the one who might identify and
offer it up willingly; to fill the void that forever lingered and at times
threatened to consume her alive. And while she felt the first signs of
stirring, deep inside where the darkness lies, illusive was his name and
anyone's guess was his game – holding the mirror to her face, forcing her
to see her self for who and what she really was – offering space for
fantasies, promising everything is possible and no one has to hurt –
beyond the invisible.

Labyrinth of Emotion

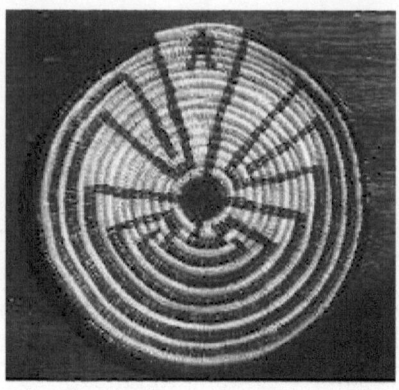

Lost in a labyrinth of human emotion is where she found herself...in the center of the raging storm, surrounded by a circle of stones in the presence of the Ancient One, is where she worked her way through it.

The frustration and anger she felt was a physical ache deep inside her soul that she didn't understand. She only knew that it was no illusion and the pain was very real. For hours she went about as if nothing were amiss; and even though they conversed, it did little or nothing to ease her suffering. She tried to reach inside and ease her worried mind, and found herself drifting further from the truth; into a web of false illusion brought on by erratic emotional distress.

Her instincts told her to retreat to the safety of the life she had known, where she felt in control; where disappointment and heartache came at no other hand but her own. Into that world she could so easily slip, where all was comfortably numb and no one else exists; free to pick her own battles and come and go at will; but her heart would not allow such cowardice and she was unable to gather the strength necessary to pull herself away...away from him, who she had come so much to count on and knew was the root of this cause.

Her angst was a direct result of his sharing himself with another, as if she should be the only one; something she had no more control over, than she did understanding. Then he asked the question and her angst was defined…jealousy, in its purest form. As she sat in silence, not knowing how to answer, for her truth is all he had ever heard and she couldn't bring herself to lie, she couldn't believe she was back to that place; a place she knew all too well, but hadn't visited for nearly two decades. A place she refused to allow herself to go, but that she now found herself in the center of.

*****

She sat at the waters edge and lost herself in thought as day turned to night; hoping that her troubles would disappear with the setting sun, but such was not the case. She knew then that a journey must be made. And so under the cloak of darkness when the night was still and quiet, she left the confines of the walls in which she dwells and made her way into the garden, where she hoped the answers to her questions could be found.

As she entered its realm, the breeze sent her long white gown billowing behind her, as the cool air wafted underneath and caressed her naked flesh; as if an acceptance of her presence and a sign of the journey that awaited. Each step taken, closer to the circle of stones, was deliberate and with purposeful intent; ignoring the cold that penetrated her bare feet. She reached into her bag and sprinkled the herbs; an offering to the Elders that confirmed her purpose and space. Then she carefully spread the blanket and took her place.

She closed her eyes and emptied her mind, concentrating on nothing but the sound of the wind as it swooped down and rustled through the trees. She could feel the breeze as it played over her body and her hair gently caressed the side of her face. Still and silent she sat, determined to reach that place; which soon she did.

She took a deep deliberate breath and held it when at first she felt it; that familiar pull that starts deep inside at the center of her self; the core of her very being; feeling as if something has wrapped itself around, giving a gentle tug. There is always resistance at first, as the soul cannot be extracted, but must wait for the moment of voluntary release; as separating itself from the body is no ordinary task, but the result of sheer will and pure focused energy. She slowly exhaled and felt her mind grow light and free, as it emptied itself of everything. Within moments all is black.

She remained inside the darkness for what seemed like hours; waiting for flight, a sign or certain sight, but nothing came; nothing but the wind, the thunder and the rain. She could see the lightening flash behind her closed eyes and feel the thunder as it rumbled around and through her; the rain as it pelted and soaked her dormant body. Then suddenly he came and whisked her away.

What she first believed to be thunder rumbling in the distance, turned into precise hoof-beats pounding the ground; growing louder with their rapid approach; with it, the sound of rattling beads and the channeled whistling wind. Lightening slashed the night sky and suddenly all was clear. She watched him approach; a painted stallion running by his side to which she would ride, as she followed her guide.

As always, his face was dark and worn; showing years of worry, torment and hard living, but his eyes shone clear and bright, as blue as any sea she could imagine; in which she saw wisdom and truth; knowing full well that the answers to all her questions could be found there.

"Ha-Ho," he spoke in his native tongue, as he raised his hand with its heavily-lined palm facing toward her. She bowed her head and closed her eyes and in an instant she could feel him standing before her. The rattling sound now louder as he shook the beads above and around her, preparing her for the journey. She felt his breath warm on her face; the sweet earthy smell filled her senses and made her dizzy, as he blew the smoke into and through her, penetrating the core of her very being.

She felt herself being lifted as if she were weightless, as if floating on a cloud or being raised by a gentle hand. When she felt the wind blowing hard into her face, she opened her eyes and found herself racing across the plains on the back of the painted stallion, just inches behind the Ancient One. The freedom and exhilaration she felt was indescribable. In the next moment she could smell the wood smoke, hear the slow steady beat of the drums and the flutes that rang out and surrounded her. She knew they were close to their destination, as the tiny flame danced on the horizon, demanding her attention and focus.

Just as her eyes locked on the distant flicker, she found herself sitting on the cool, hard-packed earth, just inches from the roaring flames, whose heat brought her comfort and peace. As she gazed at the dancing flames their color subtly changed from orange to a purplish hue; and in that moment, she saw the faces of many Ancient Ones looking back at her from inside the flames. Faces of people she had never before seen, but who seemed so familiar. She felt a deep reverberation and a ringing in her ears and suddenly all was calm; and then he spoke.

"Reflections of the spirit you touch cannot mirror your own will. Ties that bind will weaken and break if pulled too tight. Freedom was sought and freedom has been found. Such freedom comes with great cost and burdens painful to bear. This freedom holds truth and pleasure never known by you.

Freely you give, hoping for the same in return. You fail to see that it cannot be bound by reason or meaning as you would have. Expect nothing in return. Purity of heart and soul will bring you closer to what you seek. Happiness is the reward; known by few but sought by many."

She opened her mouth to speak, but was silenced as he answered her unspoken question. "No sadness lives in your heart; only lingers in your mind. Along this path you do not travel alone. Accept what is given as freely as you give. Do not attempt to take what is not offered."

*****

As she absorbed the meaning of these words, she sat silent, listening to the crackling and hissing of the fire, as the heat from the flames threatened to consume her. In the distance she heard a familiar voice chanting; one she would recognize anywhere. Her heart swelled, from the smile that filled her from the inside out; she felt a renewed sense of self and a mental clarity that had been clouded by unwarranted selfishness and greed. And as she gazed through the flames she saw him there; her warrior with which she has found a connection. Free of his earthly bonds and inhibitions, he danced in a circle to the beat of the drums and rhythm of the flutes and in that moment when his souls was surrendered, she saw his spirit soar, as his chants rang out and called her home.

She felt herself falling; her body giving a sudden jolt upon re-entry. Her eyes flickered open and the water that had gathered on her lashes stung her eyes; she wiped at them with her trembling fingers. As always she was drained and exhausted from the journey, made even more so by the storm that she was forced to travel through in order to find her way. But she had found her way, and as she stood with her wet gown clinging to her body, causing her to shiver as the rain continued to pour over her, feeling like a million needles piercing her flesh, she knew the result far outweighed the momentary discomfort; and that into her secret garden she would willingly take him, as often as he wanted to go. Expecting nothing in return.

Killer Ending

Always when the trees were naked and vulnerable against the long dark cloud of winter, did she rear her menacing head, tormenting and taunting, for really, what else was there? She certainly wasn't welcome, though she needed no invitation. It was her right to come and go at will. She brought nothing to the table but empty promises and delusions of grandeur, while I clung desperately to bygone days and happier times. This visit, however, was of a different nature; her purpose and intent clear as the shard of broken crystal she offered in solution. End the pain and reunite with the pleasure that you track like a ghost through the fog. She whispered in my ear; as the candles flame reflected in the glass and offered promise and hope that had long since been forgotten. Wicked, wicked sister; always with an eye for the illusive, while I grasp for control and self preservation. Why fight it, take it and be done, lest he be gone and all this misery you suffer is for naught. Walk through the fog one last time and meet your ghost on the other side of the clearing. He waits for you, you know. Just as he said he would. I've seen him, she says. Spoke with him even. He's tired of waiting while you make up your mind. Her words echoed in my mind, as did her screams; as I reach with a trembling hand, rip the shard from her grasp and cut the flesh while the blood doest spill. She disappears and he is not there. Only my reflection in the mirror, two halves of the same whole; the wild and wicked, searching for escape while trying to forge; and the lost and lonely, wandering aimlessly, trying so very hard to remember.

Silver Fox

Harrison Craddock was facing a significant milestone in his life, but instead of celebrating and taking it in graceful stride he was obsessing and allowing it to consume him. In just a few short weeks he would turn 50, and while generally it's the so-called fairer sex that becomes consumed with the passage of time, for Harrison, his 50th birthday held nothing but fear and uncertainty. He knew full well the reasoning behind his obsession; the fact that his beautiful wife, Emelia, was 20 years his junior.

In the beginning of their relationship, her admiration and ardor was flattering and bolstered his ego to monumental proportions, but oddly, as the years passed, the age gap between them could no longer be ignored. It was as if time was carrying him along and leaving her behind. The man she once looked on as mature, handsome and wise, now had thinning hair, love handles and the makings of a double-chin. How could she possibly look on him as anything but old?

It was no trick of his imagination; he saw the way she looked at the young men who frequented the club, with their tanned, toned bodies and carefree, reckless attitudes. Miles McCain for instance; who was closer to Emelia's age and wasn't above doing something about her wandering eye and flirtatious behavior. It got to the point that Harrison dreaded going to the club, and for months had come up with one excuse after another to keep from having to do so. But he need not be present, as he had faithful friends who were more than happy to keep him abreast of the going's-on where Emelia was concerned.

In fact, it was the last call from Charlie, the valet at the club that really did him in. While Harrison was at the office, slaving away for his father-in-law, Emelia was seen lunching with Miles and leaving the club with him afterward. It was just too much!

He loved her, undoubtedly, but he would not sit idly by and let her destroy his life, and make a fool of him in the process. He had too much at stake and knew if anything were to go awry in their marriage that he would lose everything; his job, his house, his financial holdings with the company and his social standing in the community. He simply could not let that happen. He wouldn't!

And that's when his thoughts took a dark turn. He'd started working from home for the simple fact that he got nothing accomplished in the office, for all the time he spent worrying and wondering where she was and with whom she was spending her days. And although she spent very little time at home, still, he knew when she came and went, she always made a point of telling him where she was going. Whether or not she way lying, he couldn't be sure, but being there eased his tension somewhat.

Emelia came bouncing into his study one morning, looking like a spring flower in her yellow sundress with matching sandals. She whirled his chair around, climbed into his lap and wrapped her arms around him. "Have you thought about how you want to celebrate your big day?" she asked sweetly. Harrison moaned and leaned his head against the back of the chair. "Oh, pooh! Don't tell me you haven't even thought about it!" she said as she nuzzled his face with hers and planted sweet kisses on his cheek.

"I'd rather not," he said emotionless. She leaned back and frowned at him. "Well, I'm not going to sit back and let your 50th pass you by without some sort of celebration. Why don't we get a small group together and have dinner at the club?" The club, he thought. How convenient for her. She can play the part of the doting wife while ogling her lover from a distance. The thought made him nauseous and he pushed her off his lap and told her he had a deadline to meet. She stood for a moment looking down at him then turned and left without a word.

The morning of his birthday Emelia made his favorite breakfast, presented him with a pair of gold cufflinks engraved with his initials then promptly left for her morning tennis lesson at the club. Harrison was sitting in the breakfast nook staring at the little box adorned with a shiny silver bow when an annoying ringing sound snatched him from his thoughts. He looked up and saw Emelia's cell phone sitting on the counter where she'd gone off and left it. It rang two more times before he walked over and picked it up. Miles McCain's name and number lit up the tiny screen. Harrison felt his blood pressure rise and immediately flipped the phone open and said hello.

"Uh, I think I have the wrong number," the youthful masculine voice said on the other end. "Who were you trying to reach," Harrison asked calmly. "Never mind," Miles said and hung up. Less than a minute later he called back. "I'm trying to reach Emelia Craddock. Is this 589-6737?" he asked. "Yes it is. Is there something I can help you with?"

"Is Emelia available?" Miles asked hesitantly. "No, I'm afraid she isn't. This is her husband. Is there anything I can help you with?"

"No, thanks anyway," he answered a little too quickly and hung up. Harrison stood in the kitchen, leaning against the counter, fuming. He slammed her cell phone down and went to his den, poured himself a double scotch and paced the floor.

Emelia returned a few hours later and by then Harrison had a nice buzz on. He didn't bother to get up and greet her and sadly she didn't come to the den to tell him she was home like she usually does. Probably on her way upstairs to shower off the scent of her morning romp, he thought. Just then the phone rang and he heard her answer just outside his door. He walked over and cracked the door just enough to see her standing at the small table in the hall, looking at her reflection in the gilded mirror. She had the phone in one hand and was busy fluffing her hair with the other.

"Well thank God he doesn't suspect anything," he heard her say into the phone. "Oh, me too… I'm so excited, I can't even tell you! Yes, just the way we planned." She giggled, flipped her head and ended the call. By this time Harrison had absentmindedly wandered into the hall and stood only a few feet away from her. She turned and jumped with a start when she saw him there. Her smile immediately disappeared and a look of what he interpreted as guilt washed over her face. "Harrison, how long have you been standing there?" she asked as she replaced the receiver in its cradle without taking her eyes from his.

He didn't even hear her speak, as his thoughts were on one thing and one thing only; putting an end to this once and for all! He lunged toward her and saw her eyes fill with surprise then fear as he grabbed her throat and squeezed with all his strength. A myriad of emotion washed over him as he mused at the various shades of color that played over her face, as he choked the life out of his beautiful, cheating wife.

She fell to the floor in a lifeless heap and he stood staring down at her for several minutes before turning and going back into the den where he poured himself another drink. He raised his heavy head when the ringing began echoing in his ears then jumped up when he realized it was the doorbell. A wave of shock and remorse washed over him as he opened the study door, stepped into the hall and saw her there.

Again the doorbell…

What to do, what to do, he thought, as panic and fear seized him. He bent down, grabbed her ankles and dragged her into the den. He straightened his tie, checked his reflection in the mirror and took a deep breath as he walked down the long hall toward the foyer. He opened the door and there stood Miles McCain with an unknown gentleman at his side and a stupid grin on his face. "Happy birthday, Sir," Miles said eagerly as he dangled a set of keys in front of him then handed them to Harrison.

Harrison took the keys and stared at them for several seconds, trying to collect his thoughts and process a response. "I'm Miles McCain," the young stud said, as he thrust his hand toward Harrison. "From McCain

Imports," he added. Harrison met his eyes, but still nothing registered. "Is Mrs. Craddock home, sir?" Miles asked. Harrison shook his head and said, "Um, no... I mean yes, but I'm afraid she's detained at the moment." There was a long silent pause and he finally asked, "What's this all about?"

Miles' smiled broadened and he said, "I'm here to deliver your birthday present. Your wife and I have been planning it for months now." He turned and looked over his shoulder then motioned toward the driveway. Harrison tilted his head and there, beyond the handsome young man he had convinced himself his wife was going to leave him for, sat a shiny silver Lamborghini with a giant red bow wrapped around the body and perfectly positioned in the center of the exotic hood; with a license plate that read SILVER FOX.

Smiling Eyes

He started out as a stranger that I'd see from time to time. I'd watch him silently from across the room and leave with his face etched in my mind. His confidence and character, a smile always on his face, made me wonder of the man he was, who for a moment each month I shared a small space.

I don't recall the day it happened, the place or even the time, but clearly remember the connection I felt and the spark when his eyes met mine.

I'd reached a point of unhappiness, from which I believed there was no turning back, preparing to make some changes that forever would change my life. So, I went away to see a man who once had been my lover, searching for the lost part of myself that I hoped he could help recover. But before I even had a chance to meet him face to face, the stranger appeared out of nowhere, on that grey, cold, cloudy day; a ray of southern light, shining through the din of my life…beckoning me home, with a heart full of hope.

I don't know what it was that made me answer his call, a powerful force of nature, destiny or maybe fate. But since I've come to know him, the man behind the smile, I've realized what I was searching for was inside me all the time.

This feeling that I have for him can't be seen or measured, even as a wordsmith, I dare not try to label it. I only know for certain the happiness it brings, and hope somehow I've given back, these things he gave to me –

The Grudge

He turned off the burner and while waiting for the remains to cool, he diligently worked at deleting the operational data that was automatically recorded and archived. Never having done this before, he took carefully written notes of each step as he went, for future reference. Once the task was complete, he used the hand magnet to remove any ferrous metal fragments then gathered the bones and calcium deposits, dropped them into the grinder and milled them until they were fine, powdery particles. This process was second nature to him and his thoughts were often elsewhere when performing the task. However, during this particular process, he paid very close attention to every detail.

He sealed the ashes in a plastic bag and put them in a temporary container. On the outside he wrote 1/7, before storing it in a wall cabinet on the far side of the room. He walked to the door, turned and made sure everything was in its proper place before flipping off the light and leaving.

As he walked down the hall, he removed the palm pilot from his breast pocket and tabbed to the file labeled Magnificent Seven. He removed the stylus and put a check in the box next to the first name on the list, Katherine Lurz.

He keyed in the alarm code and waited for the beep that indicated he now had 31 seconds to leave the crematorium. As he pushed open the door, a blast of cool air hit him hard in the face and made him draw in a quick breath. He realized, as he walked across the lot toward the funeral home, that although his goal had been attained, it was all rather anti-climactic. Yes, he'd gotten revenge, but it didn't appease him. It was all too quick and easy, too cut and dry if you will. Perhaps the next time, he'd have to draw the process out a little longer, not use quite so much chloroform.

As it was, she hadn't even known what hit her, much less that her death was eminent. Yes, that was where he'd gone wrong. A mistake he wouldn't make again. It was important to him that they suffer, just as he has suffered. It was important that they pay for what they had done and know that death had come calling; and its name and face was his.

He walked through the back door of the funeral home and made his way to his office. As he was checking his messages, penciling in a consultation for the following day, the intercom sounded. "Calvin, dinner will be ready in fifteen minutes."

"I'll be right there honey," he answered without looking up from his appointment book.

Emptiness of a Yearning Heart

Following his lead in the hope of arriving at a plateau of understanding that will satisfy the yearning that lingers and torments her soul; she has distanced herself, just as he. For as many times as her heart lay unveiled before him, his remains locked away, hidden from her desperate grasp, as he would have it be; and still she knows for naught, why he will not let her see.

Is it because his feelings do not reflect those which she has bestowed upon him; the white knight gallantly refraining from wounding the heart of this lady who appears lost upon his door; certain the truth would be more painful than the hopelessness of not knowing; or does his heart reflect her amour and the pain of its truth more than he himself can bear;

For all the yearning of eager hearts, can never be loved with wild abandon, that which does belong to another —

Inner Voice

I don't know why I did it. I suppose because all my friends were and I was tired of the whole hook-up thing, looking for something a bit more permanent, but still.

I should have known, while standing before the alter of the church that I grew up in, as thunder rumbled and shook the entire sanctuary, the lights went out and all that was left were the flickering flames of the candles and violent flashes of lightening illuminating the stained-glass windows, that God was trying to tell me something.

But still I didn't listen.

Our honeymoon was an extended weekend at a Kentucky resort where they were holding his family reunion. Not my idea of the perfect honeymoon, but the price was right, the ride was free and it got us out of the city for a few days.

I should have known when he passed out drunk on our wedding night and I spent the night in the spare bed watching videos on MTV, but I shrugged it off and let it go. I didn't even flinch when the next morning at breakfast I was introduced to Aunt Pat, who just 6 months before had been Uncle Pat. I was, however, the one who passed out drunk the second night.

I didn't mind that it was my apartment we lived in, but after a few months of being the sole supporter, I started to get a little concerned. But as soon as I voiced my concerns he marched his tight little ass right across the street and landed himself a job at the Gentleman's Club on the wait staff, part time, minimum wage with tips and still I didn't listen.

I was mortified at the annual Christmas party given by my employer, when he screamed at the top of his lungs, in a crowded room of rich, prominent doctors, as the family's Welsh corgi wandered past, "Oh, fuck, that dog just bit me!" And the time at Symphony Hall, when he showed up late, tanked and proceeded to yell my name as he staggered down the center isle during the opening scene of the ballet. That was the last social function he ever attended with me.

I put my foot down hard after coming home from work three days in a row and finding him shooting the shit and half lit, with an apartment full of strange men in matching black-tie uniforms that he'd brought home from work with him. He threw a little tantrum that lasted for about a minute, but then it never happened again after that.

I ripped his ass the first time he worked a wedding party that ran late into the night and instead of coming home he went home with one of the guys and spent the night. That's when something inside told me I better start listening.

I listened to him when he said he knew this great club, just a few blocks from the apartment that was having a fantastic New Year's party. I listened to the masculine roar of the pretty crowd, as one drag queen after another came out on stage to perform. I even listened after he got shitty drunk with the "girls" and confessed on the way home that he'd let a guy blow him off, for cash he desperately needed, a year or so before we met.

That night I sat in my overstuffed chair in the bedroom corner while he slept; my big blue Maglite flashlight in hand, the one my dad gave me when I first moved away from home that doubled as a weapon; and I listened to the sound of his breathing; a sound that made my stomach turn.

For hours I contemplated the angle in which I would have to hit him and the force necessary to land one fatal blow. But then what about the body…

The next morning, by the time he dragged his hung-over, faggot ass out of bed, I had his 2 bags and guitar packed and a one-way Greyhound ticket to Connecticut, where his brother lived. I'd already called, told him what was up and when to expect him. He wasn't a bit surprised; that I was kicking him out or that I had reason to believe his brother was gay. He was only surprised that it took me this long to do both – figure it out and kick his ass out.

He begged, pleaded and wept like a child, but I didn't listen to a single word he said. Nor did I listen to the hours of messages he left on my machine once he got there and for months thereafter.

My employer was gracious enough to test me for every disease known to man, and with the relief of knowing that he hadn't infected me with anything, the only thing left was to get him to sign the divorce papers, which he eventually did, but not without resistance.

Moral of this story; Listen to your inner voice…we're equipped with them for a reason!

Some Times

Sometimes I just
Want to scream
The truth of others
Too much to take

Zero tolerance
Lack of character
Human ignorance
Me mentality

People spewing
Meaningless words
No forethought
No consideration
To consequential results

Self-centered nature
Tunnel vision
Unable to see
Beyond themselves

Timeless

Dancing moss in the gentle breeze, the scent of wisteria blossoms intoxicatingly sweet; she breathes deep, inhaling natures perfume, until she feels her self becoming weak.

Strolling the maze with a silk dress on, feeling carefree as the day wears on; southern sun warming her skin, stirring some desire that lingers within.

No restraints and nothing but time; her mind does wander, the same place every time. A moment captured, locked in her mind, she tries to get past it, closes her eyes. The memory becomes real, visions flash in her mind; his lips on her neck – eager caresses – soft sighs.

Feeling it start all over again, she opens her eyes, forcing it from her mind; realizing she was about to become lost, she tells herself it wasn't real; taking slow deep breaths, as she tries to calm her racing heart.

Modus Operandi

Her muse was screaming, tired of being ignored and neglected; demanding attention, as it pulled her out of hers and slowly unfolded his world inside her mind. She couldn't steal herself away as she would have liked; submerging herself in her thoughts, locking herself away from the outside world and its interferences, as she reveled in this newfound epiphany; and so she did the only thing she could, making sure she hit every red light on the way to the office, as her pen fervently scribbled words on paper, scraps that she had dug from between the seats.

She was familiar with his work, had been for a few years, and while his claim to fiction was evident, she couldn't help but feel, deep down inside, that the words she read were real; dark, straight-forward, sometimes mysterious words that never ceased to bring her pause, as she slowly absorbed, reading between the lines of their meaning.

His profile gave no specific details, although hints of his true self it did reveal; if one were to believe he was a person of no consequence and no one you'd really care to know; which made her want to know him all the more. She read once in a comment that he was thirty-something, but found this hard to believe, as every vibe she picked up screamed older and distinguished, with decades of life experiences from which to draw.

Regardless, given his obvious level of intellect, one could safely assume that he had, perhaps, dabbled at some point, within the upper echelon of intelligentsia; which gave his calculated prose even more weight in truth to her.

He'd come around on whims, leaving comments when inspired to do so, as if sensing her absence and drawing her back, always to something that shocked and amazed her, but this was his modus operandi; scouring the web for talented writers, looking for the one worthy of telling his story, once he carried out the heinous deeds he'd eloquently written for the world to see, in the form of fiction and creative expression.

When in truth, his hermitage was strategically planned, so that within the walls of his modest dwelling, nestled in the woods along the creek, at the end of the lane where no one would suspect, he could carry out his darkest deeds, ridding the world of demons, in the form of human predators; the ones that possess not a shred of decency or regard for human life; killing for the thrill and momentary delusion of power the act brings. The ones that live among us and go undetected; the ones that need to be hunted, profiled, locked up and studied, before even one innocent life is lost at their hand.

He silently studies all those who cross his path, peeling away their mask in passing, gazing into the windows of their soul; searching for beasts that need slaying, while his own mask remains completely undetected.

That Smell

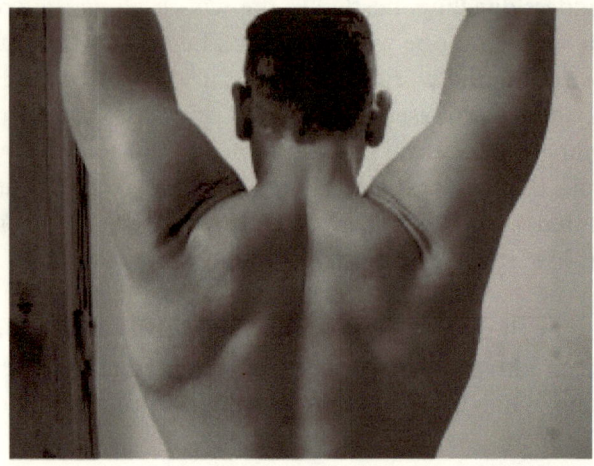

I loved his body, more than any man I've ever known; the way it felt and made me feel, especially the weight of it on top of me. Soft skin over hard, toned muscles, the natural musky scent that was all male, all his and that I can still smell if I close my eyes and remember. He was a manly man, but could be tender and gentle when his libido allowed him to slow down and savor. I admired his commitment to fitness and would have loved to sit and watch as he worked it in the gym. The day I voiced this for the first time he skipped the showers and returned to the office in sweat-stained workout clothes; claiming to be running behind and not having time, but pausing long enough for me to eat him alive; obviously pre-planned for my benefit. Silly things he did to woo me, stroking his ego in the process with my reactions. I miss that game of give and take, tit-for-tat that we played so well, and I cannot help but wonder what kind of playmate she makes.

In Silence

In our silence you turned and asked
What is it that you're thinking...
I'm glad I'm here with you
You said you were too
In our silence you turned and asked
What is it that you're thinking...
How much I love you
Wishing it didn't bother you
In our silence you didn't ask
What it was that I was thinking...
To drive with you forever
To see where time might take us-

Convincing

Although the evidence was damning, he plead innocent each and every time. As if she were simply slipping in when we were gone and planting the stuff for me to find. It wasn't just the obvious though, it was things that I found while snooping, and I'm very good at snooping. Of course those things were never brought to his attention, lest he know I was on to him and move his hiding place! I knew she was there before me, but I assumed he had finished with her long before I came along. Just as I assumed she was the only one. I'd seen pictures of others, but thought nothing of it, as I too had a stash of old photos that I kept for sentimental reasons. It wasn't until I sat center-stage, front row, facing the coffin that I realized what a good job I'd done of convincing myself; as they lined up and proceeded to pay their respects; one broken-hearted whore after another.

Raindrops Fall

The room was dark, but for the slash of soft light that came from the hall and barely lit one corner, but still, it was just enough so that she could see him laying in the middle of the bed, stripped of everything but a clean white top sheet and wicked grin. The scent of sandalwood permeated the air and stirred her senses, as she stood in silence and looked at him. He beckoned with nothing more than a slight movement of his hand and she went to him without pause. The rest of the world ceased to exist, as the only thing that mattered was what they shared in that room, right then, right there. With him, she discovered a world without boundaries and in it she was safe; free to be nothing more than herself. Anything more would have been a waste and nothing else was required. Just the two of them, free to give and take at will, knowing that these shared moments would sustain them while separated, until the next time they came together and became what they were in the presence of each other. Better somehow together, than when they were apart; different, in the depth of their connection and the understanding of themselves, each other, the world as a whole and their place in it. He held her close as the thunder rumbled in the distance and she wished she could simply close her eyes and be gone. Yes, those stolen moments…how very precious they were, she thought, as she lost herself in his embrace. The light turned green. The car behind her blared its horn. She slowly pulled forward; in traffic, as in life. Her tears falling like the raindrops on her windshield.

Where's Tristen?

Everything is in boxes. What furniture hasn't already been given away is being loaded on the trailer. She is crying because she doesn't know what it means when they say that Mimi is moving away, and no one will take the time to explain it to her. She is only 4-years-old, but she is not an idiot.

Lost in confusion and misery, she goes to the far corner of the yard and sits along the fence pulling weeds and wiping the tears from her eyes. They yell at her to stop, but that only makes it worse. Minutes pass, more boxes are moved, shouts are exchanged as no one is enjoying this moving day, and slowly she gets up and wanders into the back yard, where she can be alone and undisturbed in her sorrow; while she attempts to understand what it is that's happening.

The next load is brought out and suddenly the baby comes to mind. "Where's Tristen? The gate is open...the gate is open...WHERE'S TRISTIN?!"

She comes running from the back yard as her mother and aunt take off down the street, screaming for the baby who is lost, and only just come to mind. They find him three houses down, along the street, crouched at the neighbor's fence, petting the dog through the chain link.

"My brother...my brother," she shouts, as he gets his 2-year-old bottom whipped all the way back up the street.

Her aunt whirls on her the minute she enters the yard. "This is your fault for crying! How would you feel if your brother went away and never came back, and it was all your fault?!" She falls to the ground and buries her little face in her dirt-stained hands and shakes with silent tremors. Trying hard to control the cries that well inside her, but holding them back, for fear her brother will be gone forever if she makes another sound.

Three loads later the mother asks in passing, "Where's Tristen?" the little girl looks up and says, "I don't know."

What fools these mortals be…

Fate Comes Calling

I'd been looking forward to the trip, simply because I wanted to get away and also because Augustine Abbey was a place I'd never been. I wasn't, however, looking forward to traveling on the church bus with so many elder members of the congregation; their incessant chatter drove me mad, as if talking was the very thing keeping them alive. I'd seen pictures of the old monastery turned vineyard and was anxious to explore the grounds. The brochure said there were guided tours, but that visitors were welcome to browse at their leisure and that was my plan; ditch the old folks and set out on my own.

We drove through the gates and it was like being transported into another world, where everything came to life and was more vivid and serene than on the other side. I knew right then that I'd made the right decision and crazy as it sounds I couldn't help but feel that somehow, this trip was going to change my life.

We parked the bus and started walking. As we came upon the footbridge that led to the entrance, I looked down and there were actually swans in the waters below. It was breathtaking. I stopped to take a few pictures as the rest of the group proceeded inside. "Better not dally honey, you don't want to get separated from the group," Mrs. McAllister said sweetly. "It's ok, you go on and I'll catch up in a bit. I just want to make sure I get everything on film to share with the others that didn't make the trip."

She shook her head and smiled, agreeing that it was a good idea, just as I knew she would.

I slung my camera over my shoulder and was leaning against the rail gazing at the swans, when I saw his reflection on the water. I looked up and smiled, he smiled back; and when he did, something twisted inside my belly. He was large in stature, at least a foot taller than me, with a boyish haircut that parted on one side. He wore kaki pants with a white dress shirt and v-neck sleeveless sweater with a diamond pattern and black framed glasses; very boyish, but most certainly all man.

"Would you like to help me feed them," he asked softly. I nodded my head then made my way off the bridge and down into the grass. "Is this your first time to Augustine Abbey," he asked, as he handed me a bag full of pellets. "Yes, I'm here with a group from my church." He towered over me and never once took his eyes from mine. "Oh, then you won't be staying the weekend?"

"No, just the day," I answered. "What a shame. It's hard to take in all we have to offer in so short a time." My expression must have shown my disappointment, because he quickly offered, "But I'd be happy to show you the highlights. That is, if you're interested in seeing the Abbey from behind the scenes." Assuming he was an employee of the Abbey and therefore knew his way around, I told him I'd like that very much.

We stood in silence and fed the swans until the last pellet was gone. He took my empty bag, folded it along with his and put them in his pocket. "Did you know that swans mate for life?" he asked out of the blue. I looked up into his big green eyes and told him that I didn't know that, but what a wonderfully romantic thing I thought it was. He held out his hand and said, "I'm Jacob by the way." I put my hand in his and was surprised at the softness of his skin. "Very nice to meet you Jacob, I'm Elizabeth, but my friends call me Lizzy." He smiled at this and closed his hand over mine.

He was very knowledgeable about the history of the Abbey, as well as the day-to-day operations; and although I didn't ask, I couldn't help but wonder just what his position was. He took me to the old monastery that acted as café, museum, as well as hotel, and after we snacked on cheese and sampled a bottle of the house wine in the courtyard that overlooked the vineyard.

He then took me to the private section of the abbey where the owners lived. The stone house was stunning and reminded me of a miniature castle. The interior was warm and inviting, with rich, colorful fabrics and earth-tone accents that made up the fanciful décor. He lit a fire in the great room and afterward we shared another bottle of wine. I was fascinated at the stories he told about the history of the place, and just a little bit drunk. And so I didn't hesitate, when he took me by the hand, led me up the stairs and into one of the bedrooms, where he made love to me for what seemed like hours. I'd never done anything so uninhibited or irresponsible before, but I felt not one shred of guilt or regret, as being with Jacob seemed like the most natural thing in the world.

"Oh, Lizzy, I know this is crazy, but the moment I saw you standing on the bridge, I heard a little voice inside my head that said, "She's come home." I looked up into his sweet face and gently kissed his lips, then cuddled back down into the nook of his arm and reveled in the comfort I found in his embrace. In a matter of mere hours it seemed as though we had shared every moment of our lives up to that point, as our conversation flowed as naturally as our lovemaking. Never in my life had a man made me feel so beautiful and wanted before. I didn't care if I never left that bed.

We showered together and as I stood in front of him as he sat on a chair and dried me, the door to the bedroom opened and woman walked in. Horrified, I grabbed the towel from him and covered myself, then watched the look that passed between them. I knew immediately who she was, by her conservative dress, make-up-free face and the long gray braid that fell over her shoulder. "Jacob, I need to see you downstairs just as soon as you're decent." Jacob nodded his head but said nothing. She met my gaze, held it for a moment then shook her head and left the room. I looked down at Jacob and asked who she was. He reached for his glasses, put them on and answered, "That was my wife."

I know it was a stupid reaction, albeit a natural one, but I fell to my knees, buried my face in my hands and started to cry. I don't know why I was crying; possibly from the humiliation of finding out while stark naked that the man I'd just bared my body and soul to was married, being caught by his wife, or maybe because somewhere, in the back of my mind, I wanted to believe that I'd actually made a connection with this man and that something more meaningful than an afternoon tryst had passed between us.

"Oh, Lizzy, don't cry," he said as he pulled me to him, wrapped me in his arms and stroked my head softly. "I…just…thought…" I said between sobs. "I know, I know. It's so unfair. Life can be so unfair," he whispered into my hair and rocked me gently in his arms, as if comforting a child.

After a few minutes I pulled away and slapped him hard across the face, then immediately regretted it, when I saw the wounded look in his eyes. "How could you, Jacob? How could you lie to me like that, just to get me into your bed?" He grabbed my shoulders and held me tight and for a moment I feared him. "I didn't lie to you, Lizzy. Every word I said to you was the truth. I just didn't tell you I was married, because quite frankly, my marriage has been over for years." I shook my head and averted my eyes, "It doesn't matter. This was a mistake. I have to go," I said as I pulled away from him and ran out of the bathroom, slamming the door behind me.

I sat on the edge of the bed, fully dressed, looking out the window, as I wrestled with feelings of heartbreak and rage, when I heard the bathroom door open and Jacob entered the room. "If you'll wait here for me, I'll be back very shortly and then I'll take you to meet your group." I sniffed, wiped the tears from my eyes and shook my head without looking at him. The thought of spending another moment alone with him, both thrilled and repulsed me.

Regardless of my mixed emotions, I wasn't about to make my way through his house by myself; not when I knew his wife was somewhere on the other side of that door waiting. Before he left he walked over and kissed me on the forehead and told me this had been the best day of his life and that he had no intention of letting it end like this. For some reason I believed him.

*****

"I don't care what you demand. I love her and I intend on keeping her!" I heard him yell, as I sat at the top of the stairs and listened. "Oh for Christ's sake Jacob, don't be ridiculous. We're not talking about a stray animal that's wandered onto the property."

"I'm serious Giselle. I want to be with her. That is, if she'll have me after this unfortunate misunderstanding."

"Yes, it is unfortunate Jacob; unfortunate that you think for a minute that a woman her age would be happy with a middle-aged recluse like yourself."

"Age has absolutely nothing to do with this. We're kindred spirits, Giselle, which is something your tight-ass couldn't possibly understand."

"Alright Jacob, lets settle this right now and be done with it. I'll be damned if I'm going to listen to you pine away for the next six months over nothing."

A moment of silence passed and by the time I realized they were on their way to get me, it was too late. I sat there at the top of the steps, like a child caught eavesdropping on her parents, waiting to learn my punishment, as they stood side-by-side at the bottom of the stairs looking up at me. "Lizzy, would you please join us for a moment," Jacob said as he extended an arm in invitation. I hesitated briefly, then stood and slowly made my way down the stairs.

Giselle turned and led the way into the great room, and I mused at the way her braid hung perfectly still and straight in the center of her back as she walked. Jacob rested his hand on the small of my back the entire time, as if offering support for what was to come.

Giselle took a seat in an oversized wingback chair and Jacob and I sat on the sofa next to each other. "I apologize for walking in on you earlier. I should have waited, but…" She rubbed her forehead, as if trying to rub away a headache and then looked at me and said, "What are your intentions with my husband?" Startled by her frankness, like a fool I said, "My intentions?"

"Yes, dear, your intentions," she said somewhat irritated. "Jacob seems to believe that he's in love with you and wants to keep you. I'm simply trying to clarify your position." I looked at Jacob and he reached for my hand and smiled.

This was by far the craziest scenario I'd ever found myself in, but instead of simply getting up and excusing myself, something kept me planted on that sofa. Perhaps it was the look of sincerity I found in Jacob's eyes, or the way my hand fit perfectly inside his, made me feel safe and gave me courage. Maybe I was still just a little bit drunk, I'm not sure. What I did know for certain, was that the thought of leaving the Abbey and never seeing Jacob again was too painful to even imagine.

"I'm keeping him too!" I heard myself say. "Lizzy," he said in a half whisper, half sigh, as he pulled me up into his arms and crushed me against him in a loving embrace. "You don't know what this means to me." Somewhere in the distance I thought I heard Giselle say, "Very well," and them the sound of her heels clicked across the tiled floor, fading somewhere in the distance.

By the time we pulled ourselves out of each others arms and left the great room she was gone. There was a note on the table in the foyer saying that she'd send for her things once she was settled. It was as simple as that. They'd agreed long ago, that if either of them ever found someone else and fell in love, they would legally end their marriage that had been over for a very long time.

The only reason they stayed together was because it took the two of them to keep the Abbey and vineyard up and running and neither one of them were willing to give it up. Giselle never believed it would come to this; for the simple fact that she wasn't looking and Jacob hadn't left the grounds of Augustine Abbey since they purchased it almost thirteen years ago. He said there was no need. He had everything he could possibly need or want right there, and he knew in his heart that one day his true love would come calling…and I did!

That was five years ago and I have yet to leave this paradise that I now call my home, or the arms of the man I now call my husband.

Mac the Knife

I once knew this man – we met in the strangest of places, eventually he came to me, or I went to him – I called him Oz, he called me Liz. I never knew his real name, nor did he know mine, but every time we were together, we had the time of our lives. He never judged who I was or wasted time playing games; he was a gentleman, a prince, a jester, a king – but he came and went in such mysterious ways. On several occasions when I'd wake and he'd already be gone, I'd find myself wondering if he were ever there at all; or my imaginary friend finally come to life, skipping my childhood completely, as adult games were much more fun. Inevitably, I'd find a note somewhere in my apartment, signed simply, *"Mac the Knife."* I took his picture once, but never developed the film. Whoever he was, I wonder still.

Boris

There was a picture. It hung above your bed. A Viking Warrior in armored glory; riding a sleigh into battle, driven by monstrous polar bears. His long hair blew in the wind, created by the force of the pull, gently caressing the side of his sword. The sleigh had no reins, yet he was the master in control. And I often wondered, as I lay alone with the warrior, long after you'd fallen asleep, exactly what it was he was preparing to face. A battle of wills or perhaps he was tempting the fates. I believed I was the one you were always fighting for; time and again you proved me right. But it was control of me you sought, when you perished that fateful night.

The Experiment

This one might be different
Pretty smart
Kind of cute
Think I'll take a stroll
Inside her head
I'm bound to find something new

A breath of fresh air
Played coy
Right at first
I sensed she wanted more
Wait a day
Then cast out the big net

Asked her what she wanted
General question
Sat and waited
She answered back too quickly
Took the bait
And dragged it to the bottom

How greedy this one was
Nearly starved
Half to death
Gave instructions to follow precisely
Which she did
Lied and said it pleased me

Thought she would be different
Worthy opponent
Against my best
What I get for thinking
In the end
She's the same as the rest

Could've played her on forever
Losing humility
Ultimate self mastery
Alas I grow too bored
File her away
Experiment number two hundred and four

On the Verge

It didn't matter that they were lower middle-class, teetering on the verge of white trash, I loved their youngest son, and so I put up with them; he with his missing arm, nasty mouth and hateful attitude toward everything and everyone, and her, sweet as she could be, but spineless, submissive and fearful of him.

Needless to say, Sunday dinners were a little uncomfortable, but they liked me, even though I was 15 years his junior and still in high school. I won't go so far as to say I felt welcome there, as there was an ex-wife and grandbaby still in the picture, which the mother secretly wished was back in the main frame – so, no matter how sweet and good I was, I was the obstacle blocking any chance for reconciliation.

For over two years I was as good as a member of the family; sharing holidays, birthdays and other such occasions, knowing in the back of my mind that one day he'd marry me and then they *would be* family, and perhaps their flaws would be easier to overlook – but that never happened.

He died instead.

And when they descended on his house, like a pack of ravenous vultures, I could see the displeasure in their eyes, the accusatory glances and outright contempt, when they found a sink full of dishes, dirty laundry stacked on the closet floor, an unmade bed and paraphernalia, both sexual and drug-related, in the stand next to the bed.

It didn't matter that he was thirty years old and capable of doing his own dishes and laundry, or that it was his house to clean and not mine, as even though I spent many a day and night there, I still lived with my parents. No, somehow it all got put on me; I was to blame for the mess and probably his death as well.

For the day of the funeral, as the immediate family filled the private room off to the left of the viewing area that opened into the main, via beautiful French doors; not a single one of them spoke to me, or acknowledged my presence for that matter. In fact, I had gone early, the first one to arrive, so as to spend a few moments, my last moments alone with him, until the wife arrived with the kid in tow, and asked me to leave, so she and the baby could say goodbye in private.

It was several days later when I was finally allowed back in the house to retrieve my personal items, at which point the ex-wife approached and told me she needed to look through the boxes before anything left the house. I was devastated; just having lost the love of my life, barely able to drag myself out of bed and face life, let alone this fat bitch in my face, who was offering to sell me the waterbed that we had shared and slept in together for the past two years. Un-fucking-believable!

I collapsed on the couch, as a wave of tears washed over and threatened to consume me and at some point she must have tried to console me, because I started babbling about how could he have done this – why he left me alone in the world, after promising to stay with me forever. And that's when she changed her tune and started asking fifty questions, making certain that I understood the importance of not repeating any of this to anyone, because if the insurance found out that there was even a slight possibility that the accident was suicide, then his life insurance policy would be null and void, thus she and the kid would be left with nothing.

Left with nothing…

First Touch

Something she thought of and wanted so long; imagining what it would be like, the first time he touched her. There would be no more words, they'd exhausted them all, yet everything they couldn't say to that point, would soon be expressed.

Would his first touch be gentle or would he pull her to him fiercely; would he stop her hand short as she reached out to touch him, or feeling her heat, allow her to feast greedily? Would his kiss be tender, lingering upon her lips; or passion so intense he couldn't stop himself from biting her. Would he undress her slowly, savoring each curve of her flesh, or rip the clothes from her body as they stumbled to the bed? Would he tease her mercilessly until she begged, watching her squirm as she neared the edge; or his desire too much he couldn't wait to be inside her. Would it last for minutes, hours or days? Would she remember each moment or leave lost in his haze; reaffirmation that she still was alive, watching him leave, feeling as if she'd die.

She imagined all the time, but knew without a doubt, it would be all of those things and so much more.

Crazy World

Through the fog you can see only so far.
Then there is nothing.

It's as if the end of the earth lies within reach before you, but the closer you get, the farther you can see. Never quite able to reach the end.

Although times I've longed to reach the end. Go to the edge and stand looking down, then over my shoulder slowly turn round. See the madness of this crazy world; take a deep breath...

...and jump

Southern Estates

Human atrocity has prevailed since the beginning of time, but nowhere so prevalent as the deep south. As I wander through my life on the paths man has cut for convenience, I sometimes sense the ghosts of days gone by and their presence is unsettling. I tried to warn them that what they were  doing was disturbing to the spirits and no good would come, but who am I and what do my words mean; to men hell-bent on profit and driven by greed. I felt them most strongly as I passed the site on my daily route, the moment they moved in the dozers and began knocking down trees. I thought perhaps I was wrong and reading too much into it, but once they cleared the unwanted trees and underbrush, started bringing in palms that offset the oaks and the sign went up, I knew I was not wrong.

Southern Oak Estates – Where the Elite call home. Estate Homes starting in the $900's.

Some things are better left unknown and kept buried where they belong, was the message I heard time and again. But they progressed with their digging and the entrance soon turned into a road that led deep into the woods where no one had ventured for a hundred years or more, and with good reason. It wasn't long, however, before they came upon the foundation of the grand old plantation house that once stood proud and strong. They dug it up and moved on, plowing their way over unmarked graves of former slaves, whose bodies had long since turned to dust, then on through to the grounds where they worshiped and lived, when they weren't in the groves picking fruit from the trees.

The Master of the plantation was a wicked man with a hunger for lust and thirst for blood; a widower with a house full of slave women who did his bidding or died in protest. A posse of men at the ready, mostly kin and all in awe of his wealth and power; whose sole purpose was to see that things got done right the first time and none of his slaves escaped.

When it came to handing down punishment, the Master took pride in doing the job himself, and all were gathered to watch these evil doings. But he went too far the day he hung a mama and her babies while the men were in the groves; leaving them in that oak to rot; as a warning and reminder to all, of just who was boss.

That night, as the full moon hung low in the sky and cast shadows through the trees, a group of men filled with rage and determination, snuck through those woods and unleashed their fury. Once their revenge was accomplished, they took their women and children and moved on, but before they made it to the property line, they were captured by the Southern Slave Patrol, who wore their badges proudly and took their job seriously; and that's when the slaughter began. Sixty-seven men, women and children perished that night, and for a hundred years their spirits remained undisturbed in their final resting place, but all that changed once the estate was occupied; and the living soon ensued.

The headlines were shocking and no one could believe, especially the experts, that natural gas from a nearby marsh could have set off a chain of explosions that destroyed the development that had reached capacity in record time; killing sixty-seven residents in the blast, while they slept with a false sense of security in the comfort of their million dollar homes. I, on the other hand, was saddened by this news, but not at all surprised. Out of respect for the victims that lost their lives so tragically, the estates were leveled and a gate erected and locked at the entrance. Over the years a few have ventured inside, entering the property on foot through the backside and the tales they tell of what they experienced while there, are the stuff that legends are made of. I, for one, believe them all.

The Willow and the River

He comes from money. Old money. Old southern money. But he can no longer recall how it came to be, only that he has always had it. He is eccentric with a flare for the eclectic and has the IQ of a genius. His mansion is grand, Italianate style; decorated with fine art and antiques envied by collectors that span the globe; for which he has traveled the world attaining, while leaving his mark along the way.

His tastes are decadent in all aspects; from the clothes he wears, the food and drink he consumes, to the cars that chauffer him, the individuals he sleeps with, and the drugs he so eloquently abuses; always the best that money can buy. Life has been nothing but a party from the moment he was born, and the only time he removed the silver spoon from his mouth, was when he used it to cook up a cure for whatever happened to be ailing him. He calls more people friends than anyone I know, yet few will be there for him in his dying days, which at 49, he sadly has reached. Yes, no amount of money or intelligence can save him now, as he literally has partied his life away.

He turns his head while she changes his catheter and looks out through the balcony doors, beyond the manicured lawn to the river in the distance. Never having noticed the stone bench under the willow, he decides this would be a good place to sit and think for a while. Unfortunately, he's too late in his discovery, as his appendages are swollen to the point that he can no longer leave the confines of his bed.

"What bloody hell good is all this money, if they can't even fix what's wrong with me," he yells. "Nothing buys twenty years time and a change in lifestyle," his nurse said under her breath. "Away with you then, if you have no sympathy for the dying," he barked.

She shook her head and he watched as she walked across the room, carrying a half-full bag of blackish liquid that looked nothing whatsoever like urine; softly closing the door behind her. He took a deep breath and let it out slowly, wondering to himself where all of his friends had gone. They'd been there each and every time he opened his doors and lavished them in his decadence, but where were they now…now that he needed them?

For a moment he is quiet, as he listens to the thoughts running through his mind. A tinge of regret at the choices he has made and the fact that he's done nothing worthwhile with his life; other than see the world through a purple haze and spend an endless supply of money that he never worked a day in his life for. He frantically searches his soul for a shred of religion, as he feels death come knocking, the knob turning. He reaches for paper and pen in the bedside drawer, hoping to transfer his final thoughts before it is too late, leaving something of worth and value behind, now that he sees everything so clearly. But beside the pad lies a vial and syringe and just as he's always done, he numbs himself to reality…draws a shaky breath and is gone –

Flesh for Fantasy

It was storming and she was hungry. He was a chef with a penthouse view offering to feed her, so she went. What possible harm could come, he was gay after all and had been nothing but a darling since that first day they met in the basement laundry room.

He'd bring her gourmet fare from the restaurant and drop it at her door on his way home, three nights a week, seven flights away. He introduced her to caviar, Dom Pérignon, hollandaise sauce and chiffon – fabric *and* cake. He was a big lovable teddy bear that told her stories and made her laugh, but respected her privacy and never crossed the line.

He extended an invitation, wanted to make it an event – dinner, wine, the stormy city for their show, so she donned her best dress and headed upstairs. The table was set with fine china and crystal, a small spray of lilac marking her spot. White candles burned all around, as soft music filled the room. She could have stood there all night just admiring his view.

Halfway through the main course she started feeling lightheaded, pushed her chair back, stood and swooned. The last thing she remembered before the room faded to black, was leaning back in his arms as he gently laid her down.

As consciousness resumed, she heard him breathing; the sound of him panting, his low breathy moans, filling her with terror so that she couldn't move. She was on the floor with a pillow beneath her middle, bum in the air, dress raised to her waist. A few minutes more and he was straddling her, the motion of his masturbation she now clearly felt. Tears filled her eyes then quickly spilled over, as she closed them tight and prayed to a god she no longer believed in.

She felt his hand brush against her flesh as he adjusted her panties, fumbled with something that sounded with a pop, inhaled deeply and expelled himself. A low, guttural groan rising up from the bowels of his nastiness, echoing through her; his body fluid hot on her skin. She stirred and he jumped up, running from the room for a towel so he could wash her, lest she wake and realize what just had happened. He stood in the doorway still panting, fear and shame flooding his senses; the room now empty, except for the pillow with her indentation and an empty bottle of Rush, lying on the floor where he'd dropped it beside her.

The damsel and the devil

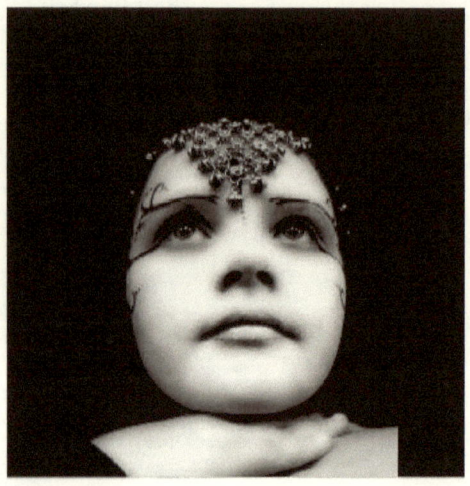

Once upon a time, long, long ago, at the foothills of the brooding Carpathian Mountains, loomed a grand, ominous castle, known as the House of Báthory. Its crest bearing the draconic symbol, incorporated into the Order of the Dragon. Comprised of Knights, Warlords, Politicians, Judges, Bishops, Cardinals and Kings, the Báthory Clan was unrivaled in wealth, power and nobility.

The aristocratic lifestyle which they edaciously maintained was undoubtedly the cause of their quest to maintain such a magnanimous bloodline. Paramount in importance and significance, inbreeding ensued as a means to this end.

Unbeknownst to them, their self-righteous beliefs would eventually pave the way for their fall into decadence, the bloodline forever marred by incest and epilepsy. Much to their dismay, this new breed of Báthory fell in ranks; producing alcoholics, murderers, sadists, homosexuals, witches and Satanists, the likes of which the noble Báthory's had never known.

Then into this world of aristocratic decadence, a Countess was born.

Elizabeth Báthory, born of the Baron and Baroness, was blessed with a timeless, majestic beauty that was enviable by all those who cast their gaze upon her. Although the offspring of cousins, she radiated such resplendence and pageantry that for a time, it was believed that Elizabeth alone, had the power and ability to turn the tables of their misfortune and restore the reputation and honor of the family name.

And so, unlike other females of her time, Elizabeth received the best education available to her and it wasn't long before everyone realized just how exceptional this child was; for her intelligence quickly surpassed that of some grown, educated men. She was fluent in many languages, when most Hungarians could not even spell or write. This did not bode well for the reigning Prince of Transylvania, Elizabeth's elder cousin, who was barely himself literate, to have a mere child demonstrate such accomplished capabilities.

At the tender age of 10, Elizabeth's father mysteriously died; leaving behind a grieving wife who hadn't the will to oversee the continued education and upbringing of their daughter;, and so left to her own devices, Elizabeth sought a means of education, entertainment and counsel elsewhere.

Unfortunately, her uncle Gábor, a faithful practitioner of the dark arts and self-proclaimed Satanist, along with her aunt Klára, having killed four husbands before becoming Hungary's most notorious lesbian, were only too happy to fill the gap left by her dead father and grieving mother. Acting as guardians of the much beloved Elizabeth, their influence and guise would turn this revered child into the most promiscuous, vain, narcissistic and sadistic killer of her time. Quite possibly of all time.

Picnic in the park

Writing Prompt: A man takes lunch to his wife's office, where he's told that she hasn't worked in weeks. -From *The Writer's Book of Matches* (Writer's Digest Books).

*****

The tension between them was nearly unbearable. She bitched when he didn't work and she bitched when he did. There was just no pleasing her anymore and he was sick of it. Yes, he'd been working crazy hours and traveling more so than usual, but his partnership was riding on this deal and she knew that. She knew it and still she bitched! For Christ's sake, he'd given her everything she wanted and then some. She didn't have to work, she *chose* to work, even though her position as a docent at the museum was voluntary, still, it got her out of the house and made her feel like she was doing something worthwhile with her time.

He'd just closed the deal in Dubai and landed stateside, with a spring in his step and a new partnership in the bag. He called his office and reported the news then had his secretary call Isadora's Café and order a picnic lunch; complete with caviar and champagne for pick-up within the hour, believing that a romantic celebratory lunch in the park was just what the doctor ordered. As luck would have it, his driver found a spot right out front and so he ran inside, picked up his basket of expensive goodies and headed to the museum, where he was informed that Samantha had not worked for several weeks. There must be some mistake he demanded, but the young woman assured him that much to the curator's dismay, Samantha had resigned from her position with no notice or reason and had not been heard from since.

He climbed in the back of the Limo, called Samantha's cell phone and got her voice mail. Fearing the worst, he instructed the driver that there had been a slight change in plans and he needed to pick up his car. An hour later he pulled through the gates of his driveway and saw her

Mercedes parked by the garage, with a black Aston Martin beside it. He breathed a sigh of relief, as he recognized the car immediately and assumed Mr. Townsend, the museum curator, had come to beg her return.

He left the basket on the seat beside him and made his way inside. He called for her but there was no answer. Assuming they must be on the lanai by the pool, he made his way through the house, stopping dead in his tracks when he saw them and realized that his instincts had been correct. Mr. Townsend was indeed begging his wife…begging her for more of the job she was doing on him! Rooted by rage, he stood and watched until they concluded their coupling, then slipped back out the front and drove off. He waited a few minutes then called the house. This time she answered.

He told her the good news and asked why she wasn't at work. She explained that she'd had a migraine earlier and decided to take the day off. She congratulated him on his success and asked when he thought he'd be home. He told her he was in route as they spoke and she immediately ended the call, claiming that she needed to freshen-up before he arrived. Five minutes later, he watched from his parking spot at the clubhouse, as Mr. Townsend made a hasty exit from their community.

"Honey, I'm home," he said as he entered the house and made a beeline for the pool. She had two towels thrown over her naked shoulder and was loading their margarita glasses and pitcher onto a tray. He opened the double doors and the look of shock on her face when she saw him standing there was nothing less than priceless. "Charles, I didn't realize you were so close to home when you called. I was just tidying up a bit."

"So I see," he said calmly. "Have you been entertaining this afternoon?" She quickly glanced at the tray then back at him, "Oh, this…Yvette came over earlier and we decided to lay by the pool for a while." How quickly the lies form and fly he thought. "Is that so?" he said. She smiled sweetly and shook her head. "Here, let me take this for you," he said as he moved in close, removed the tray from her hands and set it on the table. "You don't look so well, dear, are you sure you're feeling alright?"

"I'm fine, just a little tired from the sun and my migraine really did a number on me this morning. My head's still sore from it." She gave him a little peck on the cheek and told him she was going in to take quick shower. He turned and watched her walk away, knowing she was confident that he didn't suspect a thing. "Samantha," he called as she neared the house. She turned and gave him a quizzical smile, as he reached in the breast pocket of his suit jacket, removed the pistol and said, "Let me see if I can't do something to ease the pain."

Reckless

She mused at the constant chatter coming from the backseat while navigating through traffic. The kids were excited to be getting a puppy, and although she hadn't wanted to make the trek on Saturday, this was the only day the breeder was available.

So much congestion on the roads and 47,000 new houses planned for development. Where will it end she thought, as she let out a sigh and merged onto the bridge. She hated bridges, always had, and went out of her way to avoid this three mile span over the river, but there was no getting around it today. "Look kids, you can see the city from here." The chatter stopped momentarily as they craned their necks to look out the window. "I wonder if Aunt Linda is home. Do you think she can see us from here Mommy?"

"No sweetie, I don't think she can."
"But her condo looks over the river and I've seen the bridge from her balcony." She looked in the rearview mirror and smiled and was just about to explain why Aunt Linda wouldn't be able to tell it was their car from such a far distance, when she saw the little silver bullet of a car careening toward them at top speed. She looked out her side mirror to see if she could change lanes, just as a blue car streaked past, so loud and fast that it made her flinch.

There was a truck passing on the right so she was stuck where she was. She held fast to the wheel and at the last second the silver car shot around the left, missing them by less than an inch, just as a car from the far left lane merged in his path. Instead of hitting the brakes, wasting speed and losing the race, the silver bullet accelerated and shot in front of them, catching their front bumper with his rear.

Rescue divers recovered five bodies from their watery grave that sunny Saturday afternoon, while the breeder realized that he might be stuck with the last pug of the litter, and the driver of the blue car peeled out of Hooters parking lot, pissed off that his loser buddy hadn't shown up to buy his winning pitcher.

Room 18

The former owners saw her on a regular basis, always with her little dog, as they sold their cheap flea market goods and used appliances. She's a young girl, not yet 20, but with a lifetime of hard living and not-so-pleasant experiences under her hat. The building sat on the corner of U.S.1 and St. Augustine Road, having been the only direct route through Florida back in the day; traveled by tourists and unsavory types just passing through.

She could sit at the top of the steps, just outside her door and look out the window on the landing below and watch them drive by in their shiny cars, as they headed south to white sands and blue-green waters. Unfortunately this also meant that hers was the first door they came to when they reached the third floor, and although just off to the left was a hallway of similar doors, hers was the one most often used.

They aren't sure how long she laid there dead in her bed, before her regular John came round that day and found her there. It could have been earlier that morning or even the night before, but one thing was certain, she hadn't slit her own throat and her killer was out there on the loose.

Sixty years later and they still tell the tale. If you were lucky enough, she'd show herself and you'd get a glimpse of her wandering the halls or sitting at the top of the steps, just outside the door of room 18; looking out the window below, always with a far-away look on her face.

A group of Nuns came that day and gathered out front, praying for her soul, after the owners sold the property and the building was being dozed. What would become of her once the old brothel was gone, could they help her cross over and find her way home? They tried like the dickens and hoped their prayers worked, but no one knew for certain, until the new strip mall was built and people started complaining about things gone missing, frequent power outages and computers crashing.

The mall now sits empty, as the current property owners were unsuccessful in resolving the unexplained issues. On some mornings when the sun is rising and shines in the windows just right, you can catch a glimpse of her standing in the door looking out at the cars passing by, with her little dog sitting faithfully at her feet, that faraway look, still in her eyes.

Infidelity

I shouldn't have been surprised, but I was. You see, even though I was the first to cheat, which I realize was a horrible mistake, I had the same trust and faith in him that he did in me. I can't say that I blame him; I just always thought he'd be the better person, refusing to stoop to my level. He wasn't expecting me, but it wasn't as if I was trying to surprise him. I just happened to be able to rearrange my schedule so that I got home a little early. I went through the back gate and as I approached the porch, I felt something tighten in my gut when I heard him talking in that old familiar tone he used to use. His courting voice. One I hadn't heard in almost ten years. Suddenly I was overcome with jealousy and rage, but that wasn't enough to move me from my spot, where I stood and listened undetected. He couldn't wait to see her again and loved the little panties she wore the last time. So much, that he was planning a trip to Victoria's Secret to buy them in a rainbow of colors. He always did like shopping for lingerie. I pictured her in my mind, a cute little blonde with perky tits and a tight ass, riding my man like the stallion he was; the one I loved with my whole heart, but had been neglecting in the bedroom. My fault, I admit and something I would start working on immediately. Not a problem. Just do a little damage control and get his mind back where it belongs, I thought to myself as I turned to walk away. Until I heard him tell her that he loved her, and I realized I might just be too late. For you see, he isn't the type to say the words unless he means them absolutely. My mind flashed back to the day when he fell to his knees in a flood of tears, asking me over and over, why I had done it, how I could hurt him this way and throw away all that we had. At the time I was happy he was still speaking to me and believed we could work past it. I realized as I stood there outside that window that I'd lost him forever, and that winning him back meant more than simply ending my affair and promising to never do it again.

Last Hello

He waited until the day she was leaving; bag in hand, making one final round of farewells; realizing she actually *was* going to Paris, before he told her how he felt. As if seeing her for the first time, through the eyes of others, as well as his own; heartsick suddenly at the thought of letting her go.

He waited anxiously, needing just one moment alone – then finding it he told her, "*I love you...I've loved you forever.*" Echoes from her dream now cutting like a knife, as he took her in his arms and kissed her hello.

She returned his embrace, leaving nothing to chance of her hunger and desire. Nervously he watched her every move; rifling through her bag, producing a bottle of perfume, spraying it on her sweater. A curious smile played across his face, blue eyes sparkling, apprehensive and dazed; the knife now turned on him, as she raised her arms, pulled it over her head, handed him the sweater and choked on goodbye.

Act One – Scene One

Either it was kismet or I simply convinced myself that he was the one, when I looked in his eyes and saw the need and want that reflected my own. I saw the shy, self-conscious man who went out of his way to stand out in the crowd, when everyone else found him arrogant. When they rolled their eyes and found his humor distasteful, I laughed and stroked his ego. While they could care less, I showed great interest and built his confidence. When he questioned his own ability, I praised his creative genius. A dance perfectly choreographed that I knew would lead to an end we both desired. And although I found him visually pleasing, when it came down to it, he showed as much grace, style and experience as that of a school boy. I knew in that moment that he'd never taken his time with a woman, never been taught how, and suddenly everything shifted.

Although I went back for more, time and time again, I know now that it wasn't because of the way he made me feel, but because of the adrenaline rush I felt when I was with him. The power and control was enough to sustain me through the endless hours of flesh pounding, groping and penthouse dialogue that inevitably ensued during the act, and that's what it was after all, an act.

I told him that I loved him, because it meant so much for him to hear the words. I told him what to do, because no one else ever had. I convinced myself that I wanted him, because he was not mine, and anyone who had neglected him for so long didn't deserve to keep him. Eventually the scene played itself out and although we now play the part of perfect strangers whenever our paths cross, I'd be lying if I said my pulse didn't quicken just a little at the sight of him.

Thy will be done

She was taken back, to the darkness of that room; the one that only lingered in the deepest recesses of her mind, but was once again, forced to the forefront of her thinking. For years he threatened, always looking for a way to make a fast buck, never wanting to work to achieve it, but believing that somehow he deserved it, just for being alive. He teetered on the line between life and death, like a tight-rope walker without a pole, and the first chance she saw to get out, she took without pause. Fifteen years had passed when he turned his attention back to her, certain she was as good as gold. But he didn't stop with her, he added her husband and child into the fray, knowing full well that they'd pay whatever he demanded or he'd die trying to collect. Either way, it was win-win as far as he was concerned. He'd walk away a rich man and be set for the rest of his life, or the men in her family would hunt him down like the animal he was. What he didn't count on was the anger and hatred that she'd cultivated over the years, for all the wasted time and mental anguish she suffered at his hand. It didn't take long to find the opportunity, as he was in exactly the same place he'd been back then, as if a day hadn't passed and they still had something in common. As if he ever really knew her at all.

She approached when everyone else was asleep and asked exactly what his plan was. He assured her his intentions were to take the money and run and no one would be hurt in the process; after all, her family had plenty to spare. He turned his back for a split second and that's when she grabbed the nearest blunt object and split his skull wide open. He hit the ground with a thud and for a fleeting moment, before his eyes rolled in the back of his head and he was released from his earthly hell, his focus was clear and he reached for her one last time.

Vera Lyn

I admired, loved and respected her, because she demanded it; although I didn't realize it at the time. Always surprise treats with every visit, and never a birthday missed. I'd sit and listen to her stories while I emptied my own bag of M&M's or picked the peanuts off the drumstick. The tone of her voice, the sound of her laughter, mingled with the heady scent of her expensive perfume, made my little head spin. As I flipped through the pages of the Cosmopolitan Magazines she used to bring my mother when she was finished with them, I remember thinking that I wanted to be just like her when I grew up. Then our day came, just the two of us, shopping in the village and riding in her shiny silver Corvette; quite possibly the reason I still love them today. All was right with the world, until I did something I wasn't aware of that made her mad and she yanked me by the arm and screamed at me in the crowded little shop. As I looked at her in shocked horror, I remember her gaze, darting around the room, checking the number of onlookers as she proceeded to yell and drag me from the store, paying no attention to me whatsoever. I had no idea at the time what was going on, only that my heart was broken and my image of her shattered forever. We didn't speak all the way home and I couldn't wait to run to the arms of my mother. My mother, the woman she pretended to be. She told her stories to a happily married couple with two small children, trying to make them believe her life was an adventure, when in reality it was their life she was seeking to duplicate.

And what of dreaming

While he could reach her, put a smile on her face that lasted for days, torment her mercilessly from miles away, she still was just yearning for something she could never have. For all his eccentric qualities she found most appealing, idiosyncrasies unintentionally endearing, he couldn't touch her; couldn't wrap himself around her and make her feel the way she needed a man to make her feel.

She knew she'd never know the taste of his kiss; never feel the weight of his body pressing down on hers, as she rose up to meet him. Never feel his breath hot on her neck, collapse from exhaustion and awake in his bed. Turn and gaze into his sleepy eyes, know if he spoke of truth or lies.

For inasmuch as she wanted to stop thinking, accept the fact that some things are unknowing, believe in the connection they had forged, enjoy the moments for what they were; longed to give freely, expecting nothing in return, deep down she knew she'd always want more. More than he was willing or able to give.

She tried to ignore those things she was feeling, fearing his pleasure and pain; yet she sat at the widow thinking of him, listening and watching the rain. Saddened that she'd never come know him intimately, longing to touch him, knowing she couldn't; illusive and unattainable, always out of reach, deeply afraid of him fading away. As all dreams do with time.

Silence Speaks

Just a few feet apart with the fire between them, she sat quietly, watching and listening; his roving eye taking in every detail, absorbing the attention like a sponge to liquid. His body and its language she knew so well, that familiar spark and sweet, sexy smile; the one she fooled herself into believing was just for her. His choice of conversation specifically chosen to draw focus to his font of knowledge; seduction mode at its finest, she'd fallen for herself. A womanizer, looking for the next big score; nothing less, nothing more.

She walked away, refusing to look back, chanting a new mantra; "detach, detach, detach."

"Are you upset with me," he asked, when he called the next day; picking up her vibe and needing to know why. "What sort of vibe," she replied rather coolly; "A sense of detachment," he answered quite simply. Not only perceptive but most sincere, "I don't like the way this makes me feel," he whispered softly into her ear. She hung her head, asking herself why; words escaping on a sigh, "Neither do I."

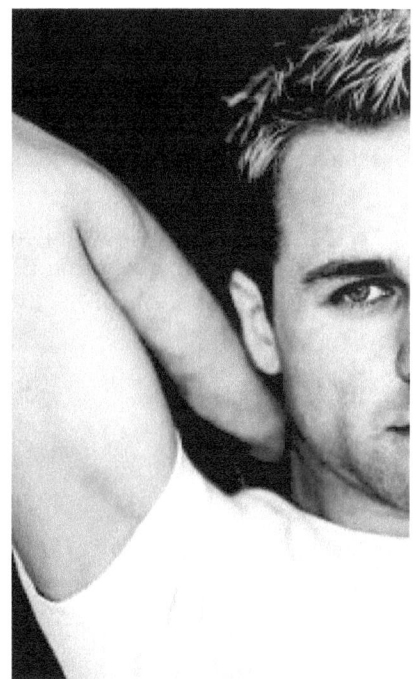

Big Fish Fred

There's more than one fish in the sea, they kept telling me. And while I knew it was true, his was the only love I'd ever known, regardless of how dysfunctional. First love has a way of weaving itself around and through your heart, intermingling sensations and emotions that are foreign and often times surreal. Every argument becomes a battle, every caress brings sudden bliss, while an embrace could lift you to the heights of heaven and keep you for all eternity. But it was his betrayal and lies that chipped away and took a little piece of my heart, each and every time he was with her.

Too right! Why should I settle for this bullshit?! I deserve better, and by God I'll make him pay. And so on that chilly autumn night, in the company of the big fish, who'd been after me for months to let him take me out; we drove past his house with the top down, which I knew was risky, but wasn't that the point? Suddenly he appeared, running off the porch out into the street, chasing us and calling out my name. Instead of realizing the impact my actions had made and using it to my advantage, my heart simply broke at having hurt the one I loved. For the next few weeks he treated me like a queen, and just about the time the big fish realized I was a lost cause and swam away forever, he was back to his old tricks and I was fool for his love once more.

Cowardly Dog

It was obvious from the beginning what he was doing. Allowing people to think there just might be something going on. She was beautiful after all and he liked the way people looked at them whenever they were in public together. Enviable eyes turning to watch the good looking couple being seated a few tables away. Even to his wife, when he should have vehemently denied, he simply shrugged it off as nothing. This not only confirmed her suspicion, but infuriated her; that he would be so nonchalant about it.

It didn't matter at that point, they were secure in their marriage and had acquired way too much over the years to let anything or anyone split them up. So, she told him flat out that she didn't care what he did, just so long as he didn't let it interfere with the family. And still he did not deny. He wasn't about to give up this newfound feeling of self-assuredness, happiness and sexual elation; even though he knew that if he allowed things to progress in a certain direction that everyone he cared about would undoubtedly be hurt. Something he thought about often; when the wife bitched incessantly about trivial things that meant absolutely nothing, he wondered what it would be like to share his whole life with her. But having her to turn to and vent to, knowing that she would be there whenever he needed or wanted her, made the bad at home a little more tolerable. He could have gone on this way forever, but on some subconscious level, he wanted to get caught, wanted his wife to learn the truth and realize that she was expendable.

Unfortunately it backfired when the evidence was found, and while his wife, his home and all of his material and monetary possession were going absolutely nowhere, he was; if he didn't end the affair and spend the rest of his life kissing her ass and making up for the humiliation. In the end he turned his back on the one true friend he had in the world; the one person who understood and knew him like no other, knowing that never again would he feel the way he did when he was with her. But at least he didn't have to face losing everything in a divorce.

Doldrums

Check the phone twice
To make sure it's on
The battery fully charged
Ten minutes more
Oh, what a bore
The moment I walk through that door

Hope for a ring
Hear a bird sing
Pretty…pretty…pretty…pretty
Glance to the tree
He's looking at me
My spirit lifts up off the floor

Intensity

Blew in like the wind
Stayed twenty-four days
Six-hundred-thirteen times
Vanished without a trace –

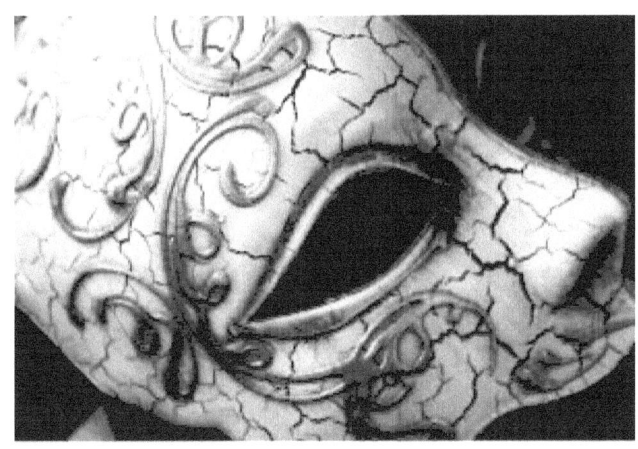

Last Will and Testament

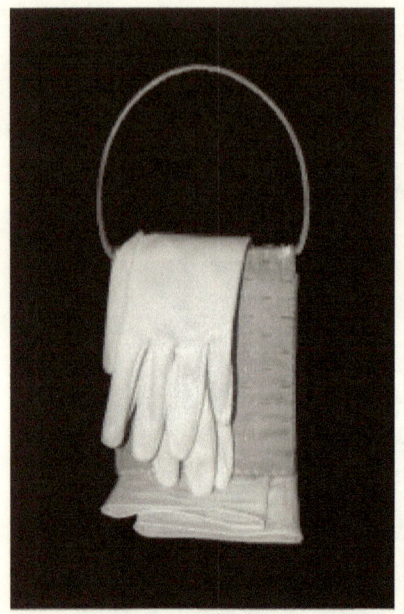

His brood was tasteless and illiterate to all things cultural, but she wasn't a bit surprised, that's exactly the way he'd been while growing up. It didn't matter that their grandparents haled from Venice and they were given every advantage imaginable; their clan consisting of well known composers, artists and literati. He only ever cared about the family fortune. He didn't want to work for it, mind you; he just expected to receive money whenever he needed or wanted it, and the sad fact is, he usually got it.

While she surpassed her peers and went on to study music, dance, theatre and writing, he proceeded to run the family business into the ground. While she was traveling the world and writing screen plays, he was busy fathering children and throwing away his inheritance on flashy cars and homes in the swankiest neighborhoods. Imagine then the horror when at the age of 76, with a lifetime of good living behind her, she found herself alone in the world; unable to care for herself any longer, and the only living relative her snot-nose, selfish, arrogant brother.

Oh, he reveled at the notion of being her caretaker, but had no idea just how high maintenance an old woman could be and soon grew tired of being at her beck and call. That's when he decided he deserved some compensation for his time and aggravation. The old bat could certainly afford it after all, with three bank accounts brimming with money that would be there long after she was gone. And so the decision was made, new signature cards were turned into the bank and the books now in his possession. But he didn't count on her demanding to see the books at the end of each month and accounting for every cent she found questionable.

Then on an outing one day they went, while the wife rummaged the apartment until she found what she was looking for; the Last Will and Testament. The brother was mentioned by name of course, but only to clarify that he was to receive nothing and had no legal recourse to challenge, as she knew he would when he learned that everything she possessed, monetary and otherwise, was to be split evenly between the Symphony Orchestra and the School of the Arts; where she had once been a member of the board and taught for many years.

A few months later some papers were brought by for her to sign; but strangely enough, her glasses had recently gone missing and they hadn't yet taken her to get a new pair. Against her better judgment, she signed the paper, believing she was consolidating two accounts into one high-yield, when in reality she had just signed her life away. Quite literally.

It was a few weeks later, on a hot summer afternoon, while making his usual stop to check on his beloved sister, that he found her dead on the bathroom floor; where she'd apparently lost her balance and hit her head on the porcelain sink, which explained the large knot on the side of her head.

To this day, long after her money was spent and all assets liquidated, she lay in an unmarked grave; while her brother and sister-in-law rest peacefully in the same family plot, just a few feet away. Elaborate headstones for all the world to see, marking their spots; purchased with her hard-earned money.

#102 Hotel Stories

She sat on the edge of the bed and checked her watch, wondering if maybe he'd changed his mind. She sipped her wine from the Styrofoam cup and looked around the room.

The gray linoleum floor with its pink and white flecks was straight from the fifties, the dingy shag rugs enhancing the white trash décor. The bed was wrought iron with chipped paint that sagged in the middle and squeaked when she sat down. She peeked under the chenille spread and was glad that the white sheets, with their yellow faded daisies, at least appeared to be clean.

The bathroom was small with a tiny shower in the corner and a bare bulb on a chain that hung over the porcelain sink; stained with rust, from the drip that had probably flowed continuously since the day it was installed. There was an old laminate desk in front of the only window, with a black and white Zenith television propped on top; the nicotine-stained plastic roll-down shade was all the way to the floor, where someone had pulled it too hard and broken the springs.

She sighed, sat back and unbuttoned her blazer, so the lace of her corset that trimmed her rounded breasts could be easily seen. She pulled her hair out of the clip and shook it loose, her dark curls falling over her shoulders; a stark contrast to the tailored lines of her cream-colored suit; thinking to herself how perfect it was and exactly what she had envisioned for her sleazy one-night stand.

She jumped when she heard the knock at the door, ran to the bathroom and quickly checked herself in the mirror, dabbed a bit of Coco Chanel between her breasts then calmly walked across the room to let him in; her heels clicking as she went. She opened the door and there he stood, in all his redneck glory; faded blue jeans two sizes too small, flannel shirt and cowboy boots. Billy Gage, the one boy she always wanted in high school, but never had, all grown up and ready to play…

One Way Alley

I'd only known him for a few short weeks, but it was New Year's and I was bored. He told me he knew of a place within walking distance, where the party was hoppin' and would go until dawn. We walked three city blocks then turned down a dark alley that I'd never before noticed. Half way down there was a steel door on the left with graffiti and profanity decorating its surface. He stopped, picked up a broken brick that lay on the ground beside it, banged out a little code and viola, the door slowly opened. A gush of frigid air, a blast of loud music and a painted face greeting us with a smile. The stage was surrounded by a bar on three sides, and as I settled myself on a stool, my attention was immediately drawn to the burlesque dancers in their risqué attire of rhinestones, feathers, satin and stockings. My God, look at the size of those women, I heard myself say. Not only were they Amazonian in size, but the most beautiful, friendly women I'd ever met; complimenting my hair, make-up and dress, while buying me one drink after another. I felt like I'd entered a secret sisterhood, where the women out-numbered the men 10 to 1 and attitudes and hormones were checked at the door. It was wonderful, liberating and yes, it was fun. I was certain that I'd made a few friends for life, until I excused myself to use the powder room, walked in and saw the back wall lined with one gorgeous creature after another, expelling themselves into urinals, a few of them turning their attention and greeting me with an all-knowing smile or wink. The scene was surreal and I felt the color drain from my face and the nausea well inside, as I disappeared into a stall and quickly locked the door behind me. I was overcome with a myriad of emotion and my thoughts grew chaotic, as I grasped for some semblance of truth and found none.

Terry 13

We led four innings 5 to 1 then faltered to a tie. With their momentum building they pulled ahead by 4, but we came back till we were down by one and continued to hold 'em. Our defense was strong and our determination even stronger, these boys wanted to win. First playoff game of the spring season, against one of the toughest teams in the league; top of the 6th, our last chance to tie or win with two men on base, two outs, and my baby coming up to bat. The stands were abuzz with tension, anxiety, encouragement and hope. Two foul balls…way to hang, two balls…good eye, one…Two…THREE foul tips…WAY TO STAY ALIVE!!! He looked at me, our eyes met and our hearts connected, I felt every ounce of pressure weighing down on him. With clenched fists and racing pulse, I smiled and screamed RIP IT, and that's exactly what he did, as the ball whizzed by and landing in the catcher's mitt. The crowd erupted and the winning team raced to the dugout with hats and gloves flying through the air, victory wet on their lips, as my baby's heart lay on home plate and the tears welled in his eyes. I could see his shoulders trembling as he tried to stifle the sobs building inside, then his head went down and his gloved hand went to his face; shame, regret, embarrassment and heartache, at letting his team down when they needed him most. He felt like a failure and it was all-consuming. Even though every play to right field he executed perfectly, one walk and a steal to second, it all came down to that final swing of the bat. Two different coaches took him aside separately and tried to talk him through it, every member of the team rallied round him and he walked away with a game ball for showing more determination and heart than any other player that night, but on the way home he said he didn't think he deserved it and was ashamed of himself. Not for striking out, but because when the teams lined up to walk the line and high-five each other, he was a sore looser and didn't walk all the way through. That's my little man…

Film at 11:00

My bus passed his shop on the ride home from work, and I have to say that I wasn't at all surprised when I saw the police cruisers blocking the intersection and the entire corner wrapped in crime scene tape. His shop sat on the corner of 8th & Vine, a cut-off point between the slums and the fine upscale retailers that lined the city streets all the way to the river. Although he specialized in fine hand-made leather goods, exotic furs and a few choice antiques, the only thing upscale about him was his address. I know this because at one time he was my lover. I was attracted to his rough, bad-boy exterior and convinced myself that somewhere inside hid the heart of a prince. I was wrong; he was just a bad, bad man.

He used a runner named Jeremiah, a local boy who longed to leave the ghetto and made himself available to run errands and whatnot. Jeremiah never questioned his assignments, he simply did as he was told, knowing that at the end of the day he'd walk away with a fair amount of cash in his pocket. Lately though, he'd been delivering to some unsavory characters that he'd rather not be linked to, no matter how indirectly. Instead of voicing his concerns he decided to make himself unavailable on those days when he knew he'd be delivering to the warehouse district, which turned out to be his biggest mistake.

Instead of getting off the bus for a quickie visit like I usually did then letting him drop me at my apartment, or come up for a drink, depending on the time, I stayed put and gawked out the window along with the rest of the passengers. That night on the 11 O'clock news, the pretty blonde reporter interviewed him on the street outside his shop, where he claimed he'd shot the would-be robber in self defense; stating it was a damn shame that the boy had to die, but if the police did a better job of patrolling the area, then merchants such as himself wouldn't have to take the law into their own hands.

He made a formal statement with the police and the case was closed. This sort of thing went on in the city all the time and quite frankly, they were surprised this was the first attempt that had been made, given the merchandise he dealt in and the location of his shop. The boys in the hood, however, knew what really happened to Jeremiah and vowed to take revenge. They did just that, the day after they lay their brother to rest.

"Local artisan and antiques dealer found dead in his car outside his place of business, with three gunshot wounds to the head. Film at 11:00"

Laying of Hands

The change in him was subtle; suddenly up with the alarm, instead of hitting the snooze twice then dragging his ass out of bed still half asleep; not fully waking until he'd been under the scalding shower for several minutes. He picked his clothes out the night before, no longer wearing whatever came off the hanger, as he fumbled in the darkened closet just minutes before he headed out the door. He even caught himself humming while brushing his teeth one morning.

He always arrived ahead of her, allowing himself time to get settled in, make coffee and check his messages. Routine tasks that he was now completely conscious of; knowing that by the time he reached the bottom of his first cup, he'd hear the jingling of her keys in her office door. Those fifteen minutes he waited, so as not to seem over-anxious, getting more difficult by the day.

He checked his watch, refilled his mug when it was finally time then strolled down the hall to greet her. Eleven steps and he could smell her, thirteen more and he'd be crossing the threshold of her door, transported to another world; one in which he knew he could easily lose himself.

She was sitting at her desk, one leg under her, the other propped in the chair so that her denim-clad knee rose above the desk. The shirt she wore was purple, peasant-like, silky and sexy. She hated the overhead lights; the floor lamp in the corner already lit, as was the tiffany desk lamp that she'd covered with a floral fringed scarf, at the base of which sat an amethyst crystal refracting the light, catching his attention every time.

He said good morning, she looked up and smiled. He sat across from her, on the other side of the desk, making small-talk and inquiring as to how the project was coming. Even as they conversed he could see her wheels spinning and always wondered what she was thinking.

"Have you taken anything for your headache?" he asked with nonchalance. Inquisitively she looked at him then with a wicked grin replied, "How do you know I have a headache?" He didn't respond, he simply got up out of his chair and walked around the desk until he was standing beside her. He turned her chair toward him, her knee brushing against his hardness, sending a wave of sensation coursing through him, wondering now if she'd noticed.

"Close your eyes," he said softly. "What are you going to do to me," she said, barely above a whisper. "Just trust me," he answered, as he stepped forward, her leg spreading slightly as her knee came to rest on his hip. He watched as she raised her face to him and closed her eyes; then stood looking down at her for a few seconds more.

He slowly reached down, his fingers grazing the sides of her face, her lips curving into a smile as he went deeper, his hands disappearing into her hair, covering his wrists and feeling like silk.

She heard the word, two octaves below his norm, as if it had escaped on its own; floating on the wave of his breath until it reached her ears. "Relax…"

He felt her head heavy and watched her whole body grow lax, holding her in his hands for several minutes before placing his thumbs at the corner of her brows; where he closed his own eyes, applied the gentlest of pressure, focusing his energy on the spot where he'd seen her pain; until he felt it slowly begin to ebb away, and only then did he release her. He told her to open her eyes, as he stepped back with a satisfied smile. She opened them slowly and immediately met his, and for the first time since he met her, he knew exactly what she was thinking.

Disco Inferno

It was the late 80's and we'd staked out a favorite club, my school buddy and I. Every Friday and/or Saturday night we'd get decked out in our best dead-eye dick wear and drive 35 miles to the city, for a night of dancing, carousing and flirtatious fun. We had so many phone numbers on napkins that we could have wallpapered an entire room. She was engaged to her high school sweetheart who was in his 2nd year of college, and still she received 3 separate marriage proposals from guys she met at the club, who had fallen hard on the dance floor. I, on the other hand, only received one proposal of marriage, but when it came to shacking up…well…that was a different story.

I saw him standing on the step beside the dance floor on one of my many whirls around it, in his Ferragamo loafers and Armani suit; most definitely not a regular, or local for that matter. I wasn't certain of his nationality, but his dark eyes and prominent features brought to mind a character from Arabian Nights; his gaze penetrating and his smile inviting. It wasn't long before a bottle of champagne was delivered to our table, courtesy of my mysterious admirer. I slipped him my number as I personally thanked him, and was surprised that he refused to partake in the sparkling libation, leaving shortly thereafter. Two days later I received a call and though we talked for hours, still I learned very little about him. However, by the end of the conversation, he was convinced that he wanted to take me away and make all my dreams come true; a condo on the river, overlooking the city was the offer he made, and while I was young and naïve, I wasn't quite that stupid. But the calls kept coming and his persistence was relentless. So, I met him at the art museum one Sunday afternoon and as we strolled among the priceless works of art, he spoke of them with such knowledge, authority and passion, that I would have believed anything he said to me at that moment.

What he was offering was to keep me. He would provide the condo and pay any expenses I incurred, in exchange for my being at his beck-and-call and providing him with whatever services he desired. What might appear to some, a dream come true for a small-town girl looking for a way out; being a kept woman by a gorgeous, intelligent, wealthy man; but I wasn't ready to sell my soul just yet. I stopped taking his calls, but it wasn't until my father answered the phone and threatened to kick his communist ass that the calls finally stopped. A few weeks later while clubbing with my friend at a new Mt. Adams establishment, I heard the barmaid yelling my name across the crowded room. Apparently I had a call and was being summoned to the bar. I answered, fearing the worst, as why else would someone hunt me down and call me at a bar? It turned out to be my mother, calling to tell me that my mystery man, Mahjid, had just made an appearance on the 11 O'clock news, as he was being handcuffed and taken into police custody, while his wife and seven children looked on is stunned horror; the charge…selling twenty-million dollars of arms to Iran.

Our truth is sometimes stranger than fiction!

Even the Deepest

He filled up her senses, all at once, like no one had ever done and the result left her exhilarated, intoxicated and her behavior impetuous. Then when she least expected it, he simply turned his back and walked away, with absolutely no regard for her feelings or that part of her life he had come to know and infiltrate so well. It took a long time for her to realize, that it wasn't actually love she felt for him; that as a friend, lover and confidant, he was in no way extraordinary. It was simply a strong mammalian pull that left her overwhelmed and helpless to control. In fact, when she was finally able to step back and look at the big picture and began chipping away at his polished veneer, she came to the realization that he was nothing more than white trash with money, and not a lot at that. Given his actions and the derogatory things he said about his wife, she finds it inconceivable that she had ever wondered what it would be like to share her entire life with him. She no longer feels that all-consuming sense of loss that she carried with her for so long, but rather pity; pity for knowing the true circumstances of their relationship, and who they really are, as opposed to what they pretend to be. When she sees them on the streets, together or alone, she no longer relives what she once believed were glorious moments in his presence, but simply stands tall, walks proud and counts her many blessings. Even the deepest wounds, time does heal.

Delusions of Grandeur

She was young, barely out of her teens and not so much in love as infatuated, with the guy who took her to senior prom then took her virginity. He was 4 years older and way cool; with his own car and apartment; until she got pregnant and he felt pressured into marrying her. Suddenly the bachelor pad that she only ever glimpsed on the way to and from his bedroom looked very different in the light of day; with the black-light posters, 6-foot speaker boxes from the 70's and the black vinyl couch and chrome & glass coffee tables. It's not as though she hated it, but it didn't lend itself to family life, but when she tried to make any changes he got all pissy and told her to stop infringing on his space. So she made the best of it and added little personal touches here and there that he wouldn't get mad about.

She'd always admired her older sister, with her big house, charming husband and three adorable kids and couldn't wait till she was married and had babies of her own, but unlike her sister, her marriage wasn't quite so happy and when it came to the pregnancy, her husband acted as though he didn't have time to be bothered. Her sister ended up being her Lamaze coach after he didn't show up at the third class. He wasn't there at the birth of their daughter either, and didn't make an appearance until he got off work the following day, and even then he bore no flowers or smiles. It was his duty, but he didn't have to like it.

She stayed in the marriage until the baby turned two, then moved back into her parent's home, after her husband showed up drunk at the birthday party. She loved her daughter more than anything, but as she sat alone in the dark of night, in the bedroom she'd grown up in, with the crib and changing table taking up nearly half of the room; no job, no degree and no plan for her future, she couldn't help but wonder where her dreams had gone wrong. And why, oh why, did she skip those birth control pills?

Remembering Matilda

The valley spirit never dies.
It is the woman, primal mother.
Her gateway is the root of heaven and earth.
It is like a veil barely seen.
Use it; it will never fail.

Tao Te Ching – Chapter 6

I'd come to the crossroads that I traveled long and hard to find, only to discover that the decision wasn't as easy to make as I thought it would be. I was given an amazing opportunity that someone my age had never achieved before and I worked my butt of to prove myself worthy. I finally had a career and not just a job, and that security and personal achievement meant a great deal to me. But there was this guy…my first husband, actually; hell bent on getting out of Ohio and moving to Florida…the land of opportunity, wealth, happiness, sand, sun and independence.

Independent from what? I was the only breadwinner; supporting his miserable ass and nasty habits, but still, the thought of finally making that big break was so tempting; but at what price?

I was 24 years old, the human resource director of a nursing facility, working with people I absolutely adored and befriended, making the kind of money I never thought I would. My entire family lived within a 30 mile radius of one another and I would be the first to leave the nest; traveling 900 miles away to an uncertain future, giving up a position that I could have easily retired from, with a man I'd supported for far too long, promising things would be different and better.

He went ahead without me, as I had to be certain this was more than another one of his whims or schemes, and for six months I pondered; facing the most difficult decision of my life to that point. I spent a lot of time alone, writing in my journal as often as time allowed and searching for answers as I read between my own lines – coming up empty and more confused each time.

Then one afternoon at lunch I decided to spend it outside, as the deadline was approaching and my thoughts were weighing heavy on my mind. My office was on a wing at the front of the building and if I chose not to leave it, I didn't have to think about where I was, or deal with the sadness that surrounded me. But I had to get out, needed fresh air, to clear my head and think.

I walked down that long hall, the hall of souls as I referred to it; lined with people in wheel chairs; forgotten people, that didn't even know where they were, looking right through me as I passed by and their empty gaze met mine. It broke my heart and for weeks I had nightmares, but as crass as it sounds, I learned to walk that hall without seeing their misery or hearing their incoherent pleas, as it was the only way I could sleep at night, do my job and survive. God forgive me.

I did have my favorites though, Bud the smoker, wheelchair bound with a pet cat that had its own house on the big front porch at the entrance of the building, always asking me to bring him magazines, which I gladly did. And then there was Matilda; childlike in her mannerisms and as beautiful as the day she was born, with long white hair that she kept in a braid that fell down her back. Matilda didn't speak; having experienced some trauma early in life that left her missing, mentally; but when you looked in her eyes, there was a sweetness and innocence that made you believe in angels. Every time I passed her, I made it a habit to stop and take her hand, look her in the eye and smile, hoping that something inside registered the genuineness of my gesture.

That afternoon she followed me outside, which was strictly forbidden without an aide or attendant, but she sat at the picnic table right by my side, and when a nurse stuck her head out the door and yelled for her, I shook my head and waved that it was alright. It wasn't so much that I was annoyed, but I really just needed to be alone.

We sat in silence and finally she pulled her nylon bristled brush from the pocket of her housecoat and undid her braid. I wasn't paying much attention, trying to ignore her presence if truth be told, and that's when she pushed the brush across the table in front of me. I looked at the blue plastic brush with her worn and wrinkled hand resting gently on top of it; I then turned to look at her and found her smiling at me. I repositioned myself with one leg on either side of the bench facing her, and I gently brushed out her long, thick hair, feeling like silk as it ran through my hand.

She put her head back and sighed, her shoulders slumped ever so slightly, finding pleasure in the luxury of someone taking the time to do this for her. When I was finished, she stood from the table and walked over to the big walnut tree, whose shade we had been sitting under. She reached out and touched the tree, balancing herself, as she closed her eyes, raised her face to the sky and delighted in the crisp autumn breeze that washed over her and sent her tendrils flying.

I watched her for several minutes, peaceful and free and for the first time in weeks I pondered something besides my own fate; wondering of hers and the life she had lived that brought her to this place; surrounded by strangers with no one who visited, biding time she didn't even know was passing her by. I walked over and sat at the base of the tree, just watching her be. She lowered her head and looked at me, with eyes crystal clear and all-knowing; and until the day I die, I'll never forget the sound of her voice, or the words she spoke, so certain; "There's no life left in this valley…go now, while you have the chance." And before I could open my mouth to speak, her eyes changed back and she cocked her head inquisitively to the side, as if she was just seeing me for the first time.

Matilda was my valley spirit; the gateway behind the veil and while my marriage didn't last, her advice did not fail.

Dapper Dan

A part-time dad who lives at home, but travels three weeks out of the month; standing along the fence by the dugout; disinterested, clapping only when the roar of the crowd instructs him to do so.

Italian leather loafers, bought on a whim, his last trip to Milan; monogrammed dress shirt, white as snow and perfectly pressed; tailored trousers, loose in the leg, but perfectly fitted so as to accentuate the roundness of his firm ass.

A family man, a perfect provider, with a wandering eye that catches mine, each time I look up from the page and find him watching me; wondering perhaps, but having no idea that I'm writing about him. Thinking about the whore he had this morning, right before he caught his flight home, as he watches my untamed curls blow across my face; just as hers fell over his, as she leaned down and rode him hard; earning her fee and already looking forward to the same time next week.

As his team left the field and I stood to move my chair, he deliberately walked toward me; smiled and stopped, just a foot or so away, as if he meant to say something. I met his gaze and held it. In the end, he did not dare speak.

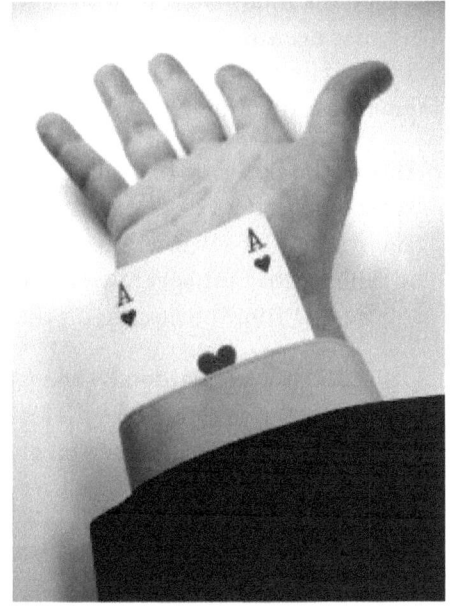

He did, however, walk away, turn and look back over his shoulder.

Misery loves company

He was a miserable little man, just as he had been a miserable little boy. He, of course, blamed everything that had ever gone wrong in his life on his mother, and while she *was* a horrible woman, with multiple addictions as well as personalities, who denounced him on her deathbed, there comes a time when we must take responsibility for our own actions and stop blaming everything on a rotten childhood. Unfortunately, he never reached that point.

Five years in the State Penn in his early 20's taught him that he never again wanted to live like a caged animal, but still it didn't change him; nor did his first wife, who saw the glimmer of good and tried to make him a better person by sharing her love and giving him the opportunity to be part of a real family. He resented each and every member of this extended family, for no other reason than the fact that they were happy and normal; neither of which he had ever been. In the end he came to resent his wife as well. His second wife taught him that a whore with addictions that match your own will do nothing but break your heart, because eventually she'll find someone with better drugs and a steadier supply. His bout with cancer…that taught him he was a survivor and quite possibly immortal.

And so the pirate of his childhood fantasies he became, setting sail on the Intracoastal, in a vessel that he'd paid for with a stolen check, vowing to take whatever he wanted, whenever the opportunity presented itself. And he did just that for several years; until the crack monster got hold of him and he was found teetering on the edge of death.

His sailboat was boarded by the Coast Guard after it ran aground on a sandbar and was reported by a local fisherman. The stolen goods that he used for trade were confiscated and he was immediately incarcerated.

Once the painful detoxification was complete, he realized that this life might not be so bad after all; 3 square meals a day, cable TV, a roof, a warm bed, a gym, a job that paid for smokes and snacks. And all he had to do to maintain this existence was scuffle once in a while to guarantee that his behavior didn't lend itself to free societal living.

All these life lessons and not a damn thing learned.

The doctor will see you now

It was a weekend like any other, and while they hadn't resolved the vacation issue, she had at least gotten her point across and given him something to think about. Monday morning she woke with the dawn and decided to get a jump on the day, while the rest of house was still asleep. The new outfit she bought fit perfectly and the pink blouse looked great with her complexion. She was feeling pretty good about herself and certain it was going to be a good day, until she started to pull out of Starbucks and saw the familiar van in the parking lot. She looked around, wondering how in the world she'd missed her, as her stomach tightened in knots and her hands began to tremble. It didn't matter that more than a year had passed since her world had been rocked; when she learned that the bitch was sleeping with her husband. No, her reaction was the same now, as it had been then...she wanted to kill her!

She pulled out of her spot and instead of turning right out of the parking lot like she normally does, she turned left and drove slowly past, trying to get a glimpse of her inside. It was already too bright out and all she saw was her own reflection in the double doors. She couldn't go any slower because there was a car behind her now and nowhere left to pull in and park. Shit!

She stopped behind the two cars already in line waiting to pull out onto the boulevard and adjusted her rearview mirror so that she had a perfect view of the door. Normally she'd sit for 10 minutes waiting to get out, but not today, not when she was in no hurry to leave; no, today traffic was smooth sailing and it wasn't even 60 seconds before she was leaving the lot, pulling away, without so much as a glimpse of the whore. But wait...just as she shifted into second gear, she saw the reflection of the sun glinting off the door as it opened, and there she was...walking tall with her head held high as if she owned the damn place. She couldn't tell if the bitch had seen her or not and at that point it didn't matter. Her day was ruined!

She immediately grabbed her cell phone and called home. He answered with sleep still in his voice, which pissed her off even more. Instead of telling him off like she'd planned, all she could do was let out a blood-curdling scream and flipped the lid shut. He immediately called back, but she refused to answer. After the fifth time she finally turned the phone off and threw it on the floorboard as hard as she could. Son of a bitch could go on his own goddamn vacation because she certainly wasn't going anywhere with him!

"Just a fling my ass! How does a fling last an entire year, and why did he jeopardize everything over that bitch! Why did I have to force him to call and tell her off; why didn't he do it on his own? And why the hell does he still get that far away look in his eyes when he thinks no one is watching?! No, it was more than just a fling and I know it! What does he think; that I'm a goddamn fool?! God I hate him; hate them both! I wish they were both DEAD!!!"

She tore in the parking lot and squealed the tires as she pulled in her space and slammed the brakes. She didn't even bother checking her reflection in the mirror; she could feel the heat in her cheeks from the rise in her blood pressure. "Son of a bitch!" She screamed, as she pounded her fists on the steering wheel.

She sat for a few minutes then gathered her things together and made her way inside. "Good morning Doctor Miller," the cute little receptionist said with a smile. "How was your weekend?" She stormed past without so much as a second glance, not having heard a word the receptionist said. When she got to her office she turned on her computer and opened the file where she kept her pictures. She scanned through until she came to the one she was after then maximized it so that it covered the entire screen. There they were, side-by-side, with all-knowing smirks on their faces; mocking her while they innocently posed at the company picnic. She sat for over an hour staring at the picture, letting the anger grow to monumental proportions until her first patient arrived; Mr. Dandridge, whom she had recently prescribed an anti-depressant, for suicidal tendencies brought on when he found out his wife was having an affair with his brother.

Fresh Shrimp & Rotten Apples

Writers Digest writing prompt; Recall your most vivid dream

I hadn't seen them since Josh was a baby; twelve years actually, since I'd gone back for a visit. We'd planned on driving straight through after the funeral, but when I saw the sign for "Fresh Swimp" on the outskirts of town and told my husband the story of my brief stint as a waitress at the local fish camp and why the sign read swimp instead of shrimp, he couldn't resist stopping for lunch.

We pulled into the gravel lot and the first thing I noticed was the addition of a screened-in deck that ran along the side and across the back of the "shack," as we always called it. There were tables with white stackable plastic chairs lined along it, apparently for patrons wanting a waterfront view. The deck overlooked the docks where the local fisherman docked their boats and unloaded their catch. I suppose it was a treat for some, but I doubt many locals opted for dining alfresco. If the smell of the marsh at low tide didn't ruin your appetite, the smell coming off the shrimp boats surely would. Not to mention the pesky pelicans and gulls that always hovered about, waiting for an easy meal.

We walked in and the air was so thick with grease that it clung to your face like a mask. My husband nodded toward the screen door that led to the deck and I shook my head and followed. A few minutes later a short red head appeared on deck and made her way toward us. Although her hair had lost its shimmer and her skin had that worn-leather look from too many years in the sun, it was Donna Delvecio, in the same damn jordache jeans she'd worn in high school!

It was a good 20 minutes before she finally took our order after giving me the lowdown on the local scene and asking a million-and-one questions about what I'd been doing for the last 12 years. My husband had a hard time believing she was a mother of three, not only because of her teenage figure, but because even though it was only half past noon, she already reeked of whisky and had a very hard time carrying on an intelligible conversation.

Donna never wanted kids, but Leroy insisted. In his sick, twisted mind, I think it was his way of making her "his woman" and keeping her where he thought she belonged. He owned the fish camp and although we both started working for him in our sophomore year of high school, I was the one that got out. Donna got a husband, a brood of unwanted babies and job security, whether she wanted it or not.

Josh was her oldest and just 2 when I moved away and I'd never met the girls, although for a few years Donna sent Christmas cards with pictures of them. Emily was the middle child and Betsy was the baby, but Josh was the one she had prided herself on most, as he was her only boy and looked just like his daddy. I honestly believe that in the back of her mind, she thought he'd grow up to be her idea of the perfect man; taking her with him, when he left this small town that sucked people's souls, as she so eloquently put it.

I remember him being a loving baby and running to me with his little arms open, saying, "Hold me...hold me," every time I saw him and then simply melting into me when I held him. My husband asked the obvious, which I hadn't thought of until then, if it was possible the reason he reacted to me the way he did, was because he wasn't getting enough attention from his parents. I'd never thought of Donna as being a good mother or a bad mother, she just was. But then come to think of it, I always did think it was a horrible shame that even though he was only 2, and such a pretty baby, that all of his teeth were rotten. When I said something to Donna about it, she'ad told me it was because the juice he took in his bottle had eaten the enamel away and caused his teeth to rot. But she didn't seem to think it was a big deal because they were baby teeth after all, and would be falling out soon enough.

Donna introduced us to the girls when they brought our lunch and at 12 and 10, they were already the spitting image of their mother; tight jeans and all. When I asked about Josh, Donna waved her hand in the air and said he was around somewhere, but offered nothing more. We exchanged information at the register and while I was happy to give our address, I purposely left off our phone numbers. We said our good-byes and Donna and the girls followed us out and stood on the deck watching after us, as we made our way across the parking lot. There were three teenage boys in the lot tossing a football, which bounced in the gravel and landed at my feet. I picked it up and handed it to the boy closest to me. Although his hair was disheveled, it was still as white as it had been when he was baby and the one eye I could see peeking out from behind it, just as blue. "Josh, is that you?" I asked. The boy said nothing as he grabbed the ball and avoided my gaze. I sucked in my breath in what I hoped was a silent and not too obvious moment of shock, when the breeze blew his hair away from his face and I saw the blackened flesh around the left side of his mouth, where his lips once were.

I forced a smile as I let go of the ball and as I turned to open the car door, I looked up to see the girls waving and Donna standing with her hand over her mouth, a look of shame on her face. Apparently the apple of her eye never became her idea of the perfect man, but instead grew up to be a rotten apple.

Only in our dreams…

Tattoo Man

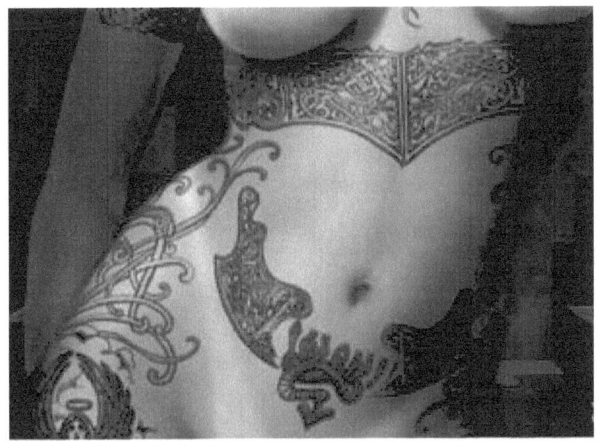

I met this man so long ago, when the Queen City, I called my home. The moment I saw him and looked in his eyes, something told me it would be alright. The first time he touched me my body fell silent, my mind went blank, never had I felt such pleasureful pain. From that day on I was locked in his spell, without hesitation I contentedly fell; until the single red rose turned into a vine, my body his canvas, became with time. These images were meant to remind me of another, but every time I look at them, all I see is you –

Star struck

He met her quite by chance when she and her entourage crashed a party he was attending in Vegas. She had a habit of that, crashing parties and flaunting her celebrity, believing that everyone was thrilled to have her make an impromptu appearance. He certainly was impressed; spending the majority of the night on the opposite side of the room, entranced and not daring to approach her. Imagine then his trepidation when she walked straight up to him at the end of the night and asked for his number.

And so began the strange and dysfunctional relationship between the wannabe starlet and her attorney.

Ten long years and not a thing to show, he thought to himself; as he sat in the darkened room; air conditioner blowing full blast from the window unit, pistol in hand and six shiny bullets on the bed beside him. He couldn't go back, that was for certain. Even if he wanted to, who would take him seriously? He'd made a mockery of his profession and burned every bridge he'd ever built, knowing full well that he'd never need cross them again; because this ride he was on was never going to end. But the cash cow was dead, as was the party and he had only two choices left.

He closed his eyes and let the images of her dance in his head, as he fumbled in the dark then flinched when his hand grazed the bullets. He had a decade worth of print and video that was surely worth a fortune, not to mention his own story he could sell. He took a deep breath and let it out slowly, wondering about her shelf life and how soon he needed to make his move, before the world was sick of hearing and he simply forgot.

"Goddamn it!" he screamed in the dark; his voice already sounding foreign, as if part of him had already begun slipping away.

Realizing just how hopeless his situation was, he scooped up the bullets and clutched them in his hand. Deep down he knew he could never do anything to further soil her bad-girl reputation, no matter how much he needed the cash. For you see, he'd sold his soul to the devil, and this one indeed, had a blue dress on.

I've got a Secret

We'd been friends since birth and I thought I knew everything there was to know about her. Imagine then my shock, when I walked past the window, glanced inside the art room and saw them there. I didn't believe what I was seeing at first, certain it was some trick of light or shadows, but when I made my way around the corner of the building, ducked in the bushes then carefully peeked inside, it was clear that I hadn't been imagining it.

There she was, propped on the edge of the desk with her legs wrapped around his waist. She was holding onto his shoulders as he bounced against her, over and over; bringing to mind the 'ride a little pony downtown game;' you know, the one where you sit on someone's lap and they bounce you like you're on an out-of-control pony and at the end they straighten their legs and you fall down? Well, anyway, that's what it reminded me of as I stood there and watched, never having seen anything quite like it before. Then he kissed her and I felt the blush creep onto my cheeks and warm my face when I realized they weren't playing a game, they were DOING IT!!

The bell to fourth period rang and I nearly peed my pants trying to get out of those bushes without being seen. When I saw her at the lockers I didn't even look at her. I wanted to say something; to let her know that I knew, but I didn't. That wouldn't happen till a few years later.

It was her graduation party and I knew he'd been invited because he was friends with her dad, but I hadn't seen him; that is until I made my way outside and found them alone on the deck. They were standing against the rail, side-by-side, looking down toward the lake. It could have been a perfectly normal thing, given the fact that there was a pretty pink package with a silver bow sitting there, but then I saw it and knew it was much more than innocent; his pinky finger slowly brushed against her hand that sat on the rail beside his. I casually walked past and stopped on his other side. She said something about the party, but I wasn't paying attention, my focus was on him.

"I was wondering, Mr. Jones, what the faculty would think if they found out you were banging one of your students, and what Kelly's dad would think if he found out you were banging his daughter?!" I stayed only long enough to watch their jaws drop open and the look of fear cover their faces. I then turned and walked away, got in my car and left; leaving them both to wonder and worry if I'd keep their secret.

That was in 1982, so I'd say I did a pretty good job of keeping their secret…until now!

Something I never knew

He didn't have to; not with a wife and child on the way, but his younger brother was drafted and so he swallowed is pride, pushed his fear aside and voluntarily stepped up to the plate; knowing full well that brothers in arms, our government would not take. And so he kissed my mother on that rainy New Year's Day, gently rubbed her belly, telling us both good-bye; having no idea if he would ever return to see his unborn babe or the love of his life.

Our life was a bit of a rollercoaster, riding the rails of his moods. I wanted to believe he was happy because he worked so hard and deserved it, and so I convinced myself that he was. How many times I watched him, alone at his best; diligently working the blade along the buffer, until it was ready to be set in the stag-horn handle of the beautiful knives that he made; or twisting the fine lines around the feathers of the flies that would catch the fish he cooked us; or meticulously sanding the barrel of the muzzleloaders that he would proudly shoot then display.

I wanted to hug him and tell him how much I loved him, but it would be years before the words would come. For inasmuch as I admired the devotion to his crafts, I was frightened by what I saw when I watched him; a man content in being alone, lost in his thoughts, in his creations, with no interruptions or outside interferences, with a look on his face that I didn't understand.

It wasn't until my own demons began to catch up that I realized the importance of channeling my energies elsewhere; finally understanding the look and the feeling of being totally absorbed inside my own mind, purging the sin from my soul.

It had nothing to do with me, with any of us. It was simply something he did in order to survive, something he had to do. Something I've come to relate to so well.

His outlet has been identified and his skills now finely honed, as people come from all walks of life to admire his work in the wood. He knows how much I love him, as I tell him all the time, but I wonder if he feels my respect and appreciation, for having put his life on the line; and making it through to give us such a good one?

Innocence Lost

She took precise measurements, leaving a two inch overlap on each corner. Once the room and all its contents was properly lined with plastic, allowing for easy, no fuss clean-up, she lay back on her bed and blew her head off with a shotgun. She'd planned it down to the last detail, but what she hadn't counted on, was her ten-year-old boys being the ones to find her. No, in her desperation to relive the pain that robbed her of her senses and left her wanting to die, she hadn't counted on that.

Several years later, during a press interview after the failed robbery, which resulted in the shooting deaths of both perpetrators, their psychiatrist described them as wild and rebellious, with no regard for anyone or anything but themselves; identical twins in every way, having lost their sense of purpose and direction at a very young age.

Some scars left behind by childhood wounds don't fade over time, but simply get uglier with age.

Valley of the Dolls

She was only a year older, but we were miles apart with a world of differences between us. We'd moved into the house across the street, which was small compared to hers; but it was only temporary, while the new house was being built. It was a lovely little house, with a big backyard and the closest thing I'd ever know to a barn; separating the house from an alleyway that ran all the way to Main Street. My parent's bedroom was at the front of the house with its own door that opened onto the front porch; a window seat where I used to sit undetected; watching her through the lace curtains, whenever she had boys over.

She was everything I thought I wanted to be at that age, with long dark wavy hair, dark mysterious eyes and a slew of boys that followed her everywhere. She was a natural-born cheerleader; one of those people who demanded attention and did cartwheels, back-flips and the splits without any effort whatsoever. I on the other hand couldn't do a cartwheel to save my life, but it didn't matter, because I knew I'd never be a cheerleader and she enjoyed showing off to much to worry about the fact that I couldn't do the things with my body that she did with hers.

We never played the juvenile games that I was used to playing with my other friends, as she was way past that stage. Instead I listened while she talked about kissing boys and watched while she practiced new cheers and on occasion, when one of her older brothers was home, we'd take turns riding his orange Honda 50 motorcycle down the long backyard and through the woods that separated the yard from the train tracks.

Without fail, during the highlight of the day, just when I was having the most fun, her mother would call her inside and then they'd get in the car and disappear for hours. Turns out they drove 20 miles to the nearest mall and spent endless hours shopping. The strange thing was that they never took their purchases inside, but instead kept them in the car. I can't count the number of times I saw Lily or her mother rummaging in the trunk through mountains of shopping bags; grabbing the item they were searching for, carry it inside and reappear some time later, sporting a new dress, pair of shoes or some fancy accessory. It was the strangest thing I'd ever seen. Or so I thought.

We'd been playing together for months and never once had I been inside her house. I invited her over all the time to listen to music in my room on my very own record player, but she wasn't the least bit interested. In fact, the one time she did come over, she'd followed me across the street and stood in the front room of the house while I ran to my room to get something. On my way out I took the shortcut through my brother's room, hoping I might get her to change her mind and play at my house for a while, but then I saw her looking around with a grimace on her face and when I reappeared, she told me she didn't feel like playing anymore and left. It was the first time in my life that I ever felt inferior and inadequate. I didn't like it. So, I did the only thing I knew to do, I started playing with the Swindell boys who lived next door to her.

The Swindell house was twice as big as Lily's, as was their backyard; and since they were 5 boys, they did fun things like freeze tag and kick ball. The first time she saw me in their yard playing she invited me over for lunch and suddenly I was her best friend in the world. I was so excited to be allowed in her house, even though I wasn't allowed to touch anything. The entire house was filled with antiques, each room decorated in a specific historical period theme. It was like walking through a museum and I kept wondering to myself where the family sat around and spent time together and where in the world the TV was, but it turns out there wasn't one, not that I ever saw.

Lily's room had a queen size canopy bed with matching bureau, dressing table and a writing desk in the corner. There was a large Persian run in the center of the room and the walls were lined with shelves, just out of reach, filled with the most beautiful China Dolls I'd ever seen; hundreds of them, but no other toys of any kind. I'll never forget her look of displeasure when I asked if we could play with them.

A couple days later she asked if I'd like to spend the night. She suggested that I bring a book since it was her routine to read in bed until she fell asleep, and I just knew she'd be impressed that I was on book #133, The

Mystery at the Crystal Palace in the Nancy Drew series, but she wasn't. In fact, she made a point to let me know just how childish she thought the books were. I wanted to go home, in fact, I kept looking out her bedroom window that faced my house, hoping that my mom would see me there and call and say that I had to come home, because there was some crisis that needed my immediate attention; but she didn't.

Later that night I woke up and had to use the bathroom, but the only one I'd ever seen was all the way downstairs at the back of the house, just off the kitchen. I really didn't want to go down there, alone in the dark, but when I tried to wake Lily she just groaned, shoved me away and rolled over. I lay there staring up at the ceiling until I couldn't stand it any longer, then I quietly got out of bed, opened her door and crept out into the hall and down the stairs. That's when I saw them.

The streetlights cast eerie shadows through the windows, giving just enough light for me to see their silhouettes. He was whispering in a soft, soothing tone as he carefully unbuttoned the front of her dress and gently slid it off, lingering long enough to kiss each perfect shoulder. I knew if he saw me there that I'd be in big trouble, so I stood perfectly still for fear of being discovered, as this was not Lily's mother with whom her father was cavorting.

I couldn't see her face, but I knew it wasn't her mother because this woman was tall and slender with long hair, the complete opposite of Lily's short, pudgy mother. I couldn't believe what I was seeing…and right there in the house where anyone could catch them! I was two feet from the front door…all I had to do was turn the lock, open the door and jet across the street and I'd be home free, but fear kept me rooted in place.

I heard things that my young ears had absolutely no business hearing and nearly peed my pants when he started moaning and groaning after carefully placing a large plumed hat on her head while she stood naked before him. I slowly backed away from the door toward the stairs and while holding tightly to the rail, walked up them backwards; one steep step at a time. By the time I reached the landing his moans were louder and I rushed into Lily's room and back into bed, completely undetected, wishing more than anything that I was home in my own.

The next morning when her mother called us down for breakfast we walked through the front room and I gasped when I saw the woman standing there in the window; fully dressed in an elaborate period costume, her hat now gracefully dangling from her hand with her back toward us. Lily looked at me like I was crazy and asked what was wrong, hadn't I ever seen a dummy before? I didn't know what she meant, until she walked over, snatched the hat from her hand, plopped it on her head then knocked three times on the hollow back of the mannequin.

Over You

I came across his picture today, and while it gave me momentary pause, the sight of him didn't trip my heart. In fact, it made me a little sick to think of what could have been lost; over nothing. And while shame and regret slowly washed over me, I couldn't help but wonder; why we do it?

Is it basic human nature or simply a character flaw that causes us to want what we can't have? To never be quite satisfied with what we do have, and to see in those things we long for, something more perhaps than is really there? Is the fantasy that we create in our minds what leads us to this longing, and sustains it? When the truth of what we seek is nothing of the sort. And if the fantasy is nothing more than an illusion then why does it affect us so –

Wives and Lovers

Hey little girl, comb your hair, fix your make-up; soon he will open the door. Don't think because there's a ring on your finger, you needn't try any more. For wives should always be lovers too, run to his arms the moment he comes home to you. I'm warning you.

Day after day, there are girls at the office and men will always be men. Don't send him off with your hair still in curlers. You may not see him again. For wives should always be lovers too, run to his arms the moment he comes home to you. He's almost here.

Hey, little girl better wear something pretty, something you'd wear to go to the city. And dim all the lights, pour the wine, start the music, time to get ready for love. Time to get ready for love.
— Jack Jones

They say there's only two reasons men cheat; to get out of the relationship, or to punish their wives. That was certainly true of her lover; who left a file folder filled with hotel receipts in the bottom drawer of his desk, along with every email she'd ever sent him, which he swore he'd deleted. It all came out in the end. It always does.

It was easy to contemplate the end of one world and the beginning of another, as they lay naked and satiated in each other's arms; picking at all his wife's flaws, complaining about her bitching and brutish ways; until the hammer came down and life as he knew it was threatened to be destroyed if he didn't cut her out of his life in one clean swipe. And that's exactly what he did.

Although she didn't realize it at the time, it's perfectly clear to her now; he wanted to get caught. Wanted to punish his wife for the separation she instigated, for the cheap-ass apartment he was forced to live in while she partook in her own affair that she openly admitted to; for stifling, smothering and hindering his creativity for 20 long, miserable years.

But especially for the fact that he caved and ran back as soon as she told him she wanted him back. He was ready to go home, not necessarily to her, but just home; to the house on the hill that he continued to pay for, even after she told him to leave. Yes, he wanted to get caught, had something to prove to himself and unfortunately his lover was just a pretty pawn in the scheme of his betrayal.

After it was over and her wounds were licked, she took a good look around and was amazed at what she saw. Well-educated, intelligent men who intentionally run away from home for something younger and wilder, sweeter and sexier. Men who love their wives and kids and have no intention of ever leaving, but are smitten and risk everything for the woman who flatters and compliments; something their wives neglect to do.

It's the lure of the forbidden; combined with the male ego.
It's everywhere and it's a recipe for disaster!

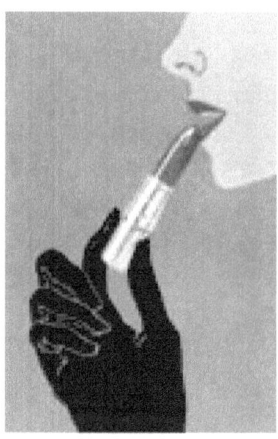

From Where I Sit

With just enough breadth in the branches, to allow its glow to light upon me, I gaze at the moon – *La Bella Luna* – full and shinning through the trees. I close my eyes, as the gentle breeze wafts through the treetops then slowly descends – its cool embrace a welcome caress, as it wraps around me in all my stillness – and for a moment I am at peace.

Hi, my name is ...

My name is Mary Beth, and tonight I'm going to kill myself; for the simple fact that I've got nothing left to live for. They'll miss me when I'm gone, and they'll be sorry for what they've done; especially her!

How could I have been so blind and stupid; believing that I'd finally found someone that she approved of and that she was actually happy for me; for ME!

I should have known when he said he'd meet me at the house instead of picking me up after tennis practice that something was up. And to think that I'd plead her case to him; trying to convince him that she wasn't so bad, just set in her ways and bitter, not just toward him, but toward *all* men, because of the heartache she'd suffered. Well, who's suffering the heartache now?!

How could they have done this to me; the two people I love most in the whole world? How will I ever get the images of them out of my mind; naked on the living room floor, going at it like two dogs in heat; and the look on their faces when they saw me standing there. Well, I'd like to see the look on their faces when they find me dead; and realize that they're the ones who killed me. Damn them both straight to Hell!

Do you hear me MOTHER…damn you to Hell for doing this to me!

Memory Holes

My mission was clear, determined in the hours preceding my slumber. A journey must be made in order to obtain the necessary information to formulate my plot. And so under the cloak of darkness, when my body and mind were at rest and the door to world's unknown lay open and waiting, my spirit took flight and magically passed through.

Preparation of meditation and cleansing are no longer necessary for me, as once they were. I simply bring to the forefront of my thinking that a journey is required, and once I reach a plateau of unconsciousness where my spirit is able to detach itself, it does so eagerly and without pause. As if triggering a mechanism, all that I see, hear, feel, taste and touch are recorded in the memory banks of my mind; for future extraction upon reentry of my spirit.

Astral flight, astral projection, out-of-body experience; call it what you will, the process is the same, though the outcome widely varies. Normally, there is a clear and decisive reason for these journeys; as the answer to a question or solution to a problem is sought. This time, however, I left myself wide open with no particular question or problem, just the need and want to visit a dimension I had never before traveled, in order to capture and create from whence I had come.

I was not disappointed, but I was however distressed and somewhat traumatized by the experience. It was as if I was being led, instead of traveling of my own free will, and the one doing the leading had a specific reason for taking me there. The reason was to reacquaint me with my sin. The destination was HELL!

The corridor was long and dark, with hard-packed dirt floors and walls of rock that were high and arched; like the tunnels they dig through mountains, only there was no end in sight.

As I was led through the center of the tunnel, glass-fronted rooms lined either side. In each room, or life-size box as I came to think of them, was a specific scene from my life; scenes of sin that I had forced myself to forget; filing them away in the deepest recesses of my mind, where I was certain they would stay locked. Suddenly, and without warning, forced to relive each and every one.

To stand outside the box and watch, grateful when the show was over and the box went dark; only to turn and see the miles and miles of sin that lay ahead; sin that I must now suffer; as no thought, regard or consideration was given at the time.

The dread I felt, at the prospect of having to suffer so many, pales in comparison to the shame, regret and repulsion I felt; as I watched myself commit one deadly sin after another.

I begged for mercy, but mercy was not given; for this is death at its inception and what each and every one of us must go through. While the decision has already been made, the process by which it was determined is played out for us; right before our eyes, in the form of our lives.

"Be certain that your sins will find you out."
Numbers 32:23

As If

I have a bad habit of not checking my messages until the phone flashes FULL, then I spend 20 minutes listening and deleting. Today I was transported to a place in my past; another lifetime entirely, and one I'd just as soon forget altogether. But his voice, pitiful and tear-filled took me back, turned my stomach and filled me with rage. How dare he invade my personal space, make his presence known, call me by the nickname he gave me almost 20 years ago; have the audacity to tell me he loves me; as if a decade hadn't passed since I divorced his miserable ass. As if he has anything to say that I want to hear. As if I have the time, words, breath, or energy to waste on him at all!

We could have lived in the grandest palace with the finest furnishings, and still there would be pictures hanging in precarious places, covering holes in the walls, as a result of his explosive temper. Those holes were easy to cover, but the ones he drilled through my psyche and spirit, with his abusive actions and hateful words, weren't so easy to conceal. For the longest time I blamed myself, fearing that for some reason I wasn't a good wife, unable to give him whatever it was he needed or wanted. I'd like to say that I got over that pretty quickly, but in all actuality, it took years before I realized that it might not have been gold that I thought I once glimpsed in the middle of that cold, hard heart of his.

Then came the day when I realized just how much I hated him, and how cruel he truly could be.

We lived in a renovated barn loft on 96 acres in the middle of nowhere. We were sitting at the table in the little breakfast nook, beside two large windows that offered a perfect view of the sunrise over the field. I'd hung my lace curtains that gently blew in the breeze and mounted a birdfeeder outside on the deck. A pair of Chickadees, male and female, came every morning for breakfast around the same time I had my coffee. It was a peaceful way to begin my days; days that would inevitably turn tumultuous with the shifting of his moods, depending on how much weed was left; weed that he'd always find a way to buy, even if it meant going without necessities. His addiction ruled his life, in turn, ruling mines as well.

He'd purchased a pellet gun, with little CO2 cartridges that powered it, spending his free time shooting at targets or cans he'd line along the fence row; believing that if he had a hobby, something to occupy his time and mind, his addiction would wan. It didn't of course, but it kept him amused for a while and out of the loft. That morning as he sat at the table with me, sun slowly rising on the horizon, birds chirping happily at the feeder, he looked at me and smiled; pointed his gun out the window and shot one of the birds through the screen, for no other reason than pure meanness.

I was shocked that he would do such a thing, and devastated at my loss. And then it hit me, he was jealous of the birds; jealous because they brought me momentary happiness; simple happiness that he'd never known and could never understand; happiness that took my focus off of him for a few fleeting, peaceful moments. It was then that I realized just how sick and twisted he was. And each morning I was reminded, as the male Chickadee made his pilgrimage to the feeder and called mournfully for his mate.

This Chickadee has a new mate and is not the least bit interested in listening to you call mournfully to the mate you killed a lifetime ago...

AS IF!

Shadows in Glass

Labor Day weekend at the Cape was an event not to be missed. The local artisans and shopkeepers all gathered together to put on the biggest festival of the year, as it marked the end of summer, as well as tourist season. I can't say that I was sorry to see the season come to an end. The tourist's descended on our little town and basically took it over for five months out of the year, and while that was good for my husband's business, I looked forward to the day I could walk down the street without being stopped and asked for an autograph. Don't get me wrong, I love my fans and the fact that every shop in town stocks my books in their own 'local author' display; if it weren't for them I wouldn't be fulfilling my life's dream, but I'm a very private person, and believe it or not, I don't like talking about myself or my work.

It was the last night of festivities and I'd made my way to the pavilion to listen to the band. The evening was perfect. The garden club had done an outstanding job of decorating, as every single tree surrounding the park was filled with twinkling white lights that only added to the romance of the evening. There was a cool breeze wafting in off the bay and the sky was filled with zillions of stars. I remember thinking to myself how perfect it would be, if only I had someone to share it with; and I say someone, meaning anyone and no one in particular, because over the past 3 years my marriage appears to have grown stagnant. Oh, it isn't as if Darren and I have stopped loving each other, it's just that we're moving at different paces and both wrapped up in our careers right now. I have total faith that one day things will calm down and we'll get back to the business of living as a couple again. It's just that at present, we seem to be moving in opposite directions.

So, I was just about to leave the park and walk myself back home when I felt him come up behind me. The heat radiated off his body and carried his musky scent straight to my senses, catching me unawares and momentarily lulling me into a trace-like state. I stood with my eyes closed, savoring his manliness that threatened to consume me, and then I felt his breath, hot on my neck, lingering; his lips cool against my flesh. A small sigh of ecstasy escaped from somewhere deep inside, as my head tilted in offering.

"Do you have any idea how long I've wanted to do that?" he whispered softly in my ear. A smile slowly spread across my lips, in pleasant recognition. I turned and looked up into his beautiful blue eyes; matured in the years that had separated us, but still pale as the summer sky. I realized as I stood there looking into his face, that I'd only ever known the boy, never the man; but sensed that was about to change.

He walked me home and in shadows of the trees, just outside my front door, I let him kiss me. Something in my belly quivered, in that moment when his body was pressed against mine, his arms wrapped around me in a lover's sweet embrace; his lips lingered so close that I could feel his breath mix with mine. His mouth crushed against mine hungrily, his tongue exploring erotically, as we sank into each other and savored the moment.

He called two times the following day before finally leaving a message. "You know it isn't good for an old man's heart to be led on by a beautiful woman and then left hanging this way. Call me Bethy. I want to see you again." Old man my ass, I thought. If he was an old man then that made me an old woman and nothing could be further from the truth! I didn't call him back, although I thought of little else the entire day.

***

We met for lunch the following Saturday and the sexual tension between us was intense, so much so that I was afraid those around us would surely pick up on it. That's when I decided to take him home and show him my studio. I laughed in pure delight when we walked to the end of the block, turned the corner and there, parked along the curb sat a red Ferrari Daytona Spyder. "It suits you," I said simply, as he held the door and I slid into the cushy leather seat, wondering why I didn't have one of my own. We drove through town on the backstreets and it was heavenly; the breeze in my hair with just enough of a bite to chill me. He reached over and rested his hand on my knee and squeezed gently, without ever taking his eyes from the road.

Even though he'd walked me home a week ago, it had been dark and he not only didn't remember the way, but he'd never actually gotten a good look at the house. "All the way at the end, the one on the right," I said as I pointed. "You're kidding right?" I looked at him questioningly, "Why would I be kidding?" He shook his head and laughed, "Oh, I don't know, maybe because it's the biggest house in the whole town!" When I didn't answer he just smiled and said, "Books, huh? Must be a hell of a business!"

For a moment I was actually embarrassed. I don't know why, I had no reason to be, I'd worked my ass off for the last 20 years to get to where I was now, but suddenly my choice of lifestyle seemed excessive. "What'd you say your husband does?" he asked. "I didn't...but he's an artist. Has a little studio on the other side of town. He's very popular with the locals as well as the tourists. I paused and then said, "He does a lot of traveling, to festivals and small galleries, in fact that's where he is now," I said without thinking; until he looked at me with a wicked grin and I felt myself blush.

"I read the bio on your website. You never had kids, so why the big house?" I knew I'd feel ridiculous telling him the truth; that I'd fallen in love with the old Inn as soon as I'd seen it and made the owners an offer they couldn't refuse; simply because it had a mother-in-laws cottage along the water that would make a perfect writing studio, so I told him we did a lot of entertaining with family and friends who stayed with us when they visited. I don't think he bought it. It didn't matter.

We walked around the side of the house and went straight to the studio. The minute we were inside and the door was closed, he pushed me up against the desk and took my face in his hands. I shuddered in anticipation of what was to come, and as I drew in a trembling breath, he took my mouth with his and explored avidly; leaving the taste of him lingering, as he roamed my face and neck. He gently unbuttoned my shirt and eased it off my shoulders; "Mm…nice," he said as he ran his thumbs over the lace of my bra. My head fell back and I heard myself moan, as his fingers continued to explore my flesh. I reached for him he said, "Just let me touch…" and so I did. I gave myself to him, leaning there against the desk, my body turning to jelly by the pure physical pleasure of his touch.

We didn't do much talking, at least not about him. He told me that although he wasn't a reader and wasn't personally familiar with my work, he was impressed that I'd followed my dreams and found success and happiness in my passion. He also told me, as we lay naked with his head on my breast and my hand playing in his mane of dark curls that he thought I was a dork in school, always with my face buried in a book. Then before I had a chance to retort, he rolled over on top of me and stole my breath away.

***

This went on for several months, him coming to me, always to my studio, whenever he wanted. Darren was doing so well at the gallery showings that his travels increased quite a bit and while admittedly I was blinded by lust, still, I should have known better.

It was all handled very civil; the divorce papers conveniently delivered while Darren was out of town. He was suing me for adultery, claiming that there were no cracks in the relationship prior to my infidelity, and betrayal of the vows I made on our wedding day. I flew to New York and met with my attorney, who advised me to sign the papers, saying that every detail of our personal lives would be dragged out in a very public battle otherwise; reminding me how damaging it could be to my career. But I wasn't comfortable with that; handing over everything I'd worked so hard for, when the truth of the matter was, I was the one who bought the house, I was the one who leased Darren's studio and supported us while he fiddled with his blown glass bobbles that brought in less than 20,000 a year in sales. It didn't matter at the time; I was happy to support him, as I knew what was involved in honing your skills and getting your name out there. Nothing worth having comes easily, but nothing worth keeping should be given away without a fight!

For two solid weeks my attorney and I strategized for the ensuing battle. By the time I boarded my return flight home, I was mentally and physically exhausted. I grabbed a cab at the airport and prayed that Darren wouldn't be there when I got home. Thankfully the house was dark and there was no sign of him when the cab dropped me at my door.

I grabbed a quick shower and realizing I was too keyed up to sleep, I decided to go to the studio and write for a while; and that's when I found them; my husband and my lover, in a very compromising position, right there on the floor in front of the fireplace. *My* fireplace, in *my* studio!

"Son-of-a-bitch" was all I could manage; as I stood in shock, my mouth agape, trying to rationalize and understand, not only what was happening, but exactly what this all meant.

I reached for the closest object and whirled a paperweight across the room at them. "Bethy wait!" Rod shouted as he jumped up. "Oh, Jesus," Darren moaned, as he rolled over while covering himself, and buried his face in his hands.

The above photo is now used on the dust jackets of all my books. It's the once coveted red Ferrari Daytona Spyder, whose vanity plate fittingly reads, Poetic Justice.

Diamonds are Forever

He waited patiently, hidden in the shadows, for just the right opportunity to present itself, and then it did; glittering jewels against porcelain skin, slowly descending the stone steps, totally oblivious and unaware, of the evil that lingered in darkness, just beyond the outskirts of her world.

In the seconds it took to process his threatening words and the reality of what was happening, he'd ripped the necklace from her throat and shot her husband dead. Her own words echoed in her mind, "STOP HIM BOB, HE HAS MY NECKLACE!" along with the ringing of gunshots and faraway screams. He was defending her honor, following her orders and instinctively fighting for what belonged to them. But it was, after all, only a piece of jewelry; and while expensive at the time of purchase, the ultimate price he ended paying, was way too high.

*****

He ran a very prestigious practice, booking patients up to sixteen months in advance; from all over the world they traveled for his services. He was the genius behind several surgical procedures and featured in JAMA magazine on a regular basis, but he was a man, just like any other. He could have had a private wing in any hospital of his choosing, but that wasn't his style. Instead he built his practice in an old Victorian mansion in Mt. Adams that sat high atop a hill, with breathtaking views of the city below; and I was lucky enough to be one of his employees.

He treated us as equals, each job as important as the next, even my position as receptionist; because as he once told me, I was the first point of contact and first impressions are always the most important. I took pride in my work and it showed. I was 23, totally self-sufficient and able to afford my own high rise apartment with a clothing allowance left over, once all the bills were paid. It was the perfect set-up and truth be told, I was living my dream.

Several times throughout the year we were invited to his home for private parties or picnics; some just for his staff, but others included colleagues from all over the world; and while his home was excessive in displays of grandeur, he showed no pretension in his behavior or the treatment of his guests. His wife on the other hand, made her position and social standing perfectly clear to any and all that crossed her path.

She made regular visits to the office at least twice a week. No one knew exactly what she did during the time she locked herself away in the doctor's private office, but it was on one of these visits when I realized just how superficial she was.

I was on my way to deliver a letter for signature when I heard them through the door. She was livid because he'd offered me tickets to the ballet that they wouldn't be using, as she believed it would somehow tarnish their pristine reputation to have a lowly receptionist, a complete and total nobody, taking their place in the high-priced seats that for seven seasons had belonged only to them. He told her she was being ridiculous and stormed out of the office. He was surprised to find me there, but graciously smiled and thanked me for the file, as I pretended I hadn't heard a thing. I often wondered though, if I'd succeeded in disguising the pity I felt for him in that moment.

A few months later he received a special delivery from Cartier, so special in fact that I was told only the doctor himself could sign for it. Forty-five minutes later, he signed and received his package and swore me to secrecy, as I followed him into his office to glimpse the anniversary present he'd had made for the Missus.

I was speechless when he carefully opened the lid to the large leather box and revealed the gold necklace with diamond, amethyst and turquoise stones; an exact replica of the necklace the Duchess of Windsor had worn in 1947. He was so proud of himself, telling me how he planned to surprise her with it the following evening, before they dined at the

Masionetté and finished off the evening at the symphony. He asked if I thought she would like it and I told him she'd be crazy not to, and that she was one lucky woman; not because of the gift, but because of the wonderful man she had as a husband. Those were the last words I ever spoke to him.

Bad Medicine

I kept telling them I was fine, there was nothing wrong and I didn't *want* to have the surgery, but they wouldn't listen. The school had sent home a letter the day after they came and tested the class, along with the name and number of a doctor who specialized in childhood scoliosis, and that's all there was to it. They had the entire class line up along the blackboard and one-by-one they called us forward. I hesitated when my name was called, not because the test was frightening or hard, but because I couldn't shake the feeling that something about this was wrong.

I stepped forward, was told to put my hands on my hips and bend forward, as if touching my nose to my knees, and just that quick the determination was made and my fate sealed. There were no second opinions, no questioning the diagnosis, despite the fact that I was a healthy, normal functioning 10-year-old, who'd never experienced a bit of back or neck pain my entire life. My parents simply signed the papers, scheduled the surgery, and drove me to the hospital, where they stole my childhood and ruined my life.

For twelve long, agonizing weeks I stayed in hospital, forced to lay flat on my back; totally alone and scared to death. My father was a truck driver and on the road most of the time, so I only saw him 3 times during my entire stay. My mother had three other children to tend to, so she only came to visit once or twice a week, for an hour or so at a time, but brought little to no comfort with her when she did come. It was as if she were blaming *me* for the position I was in, as if *I'd* done something wrong. "Always slouching and shuffling your feet, and this is what's come of it," she'd say in that condescending tone. The nurses were nice enough though and eventually I was moved from my private room into a dormitory style wing, with other children in various stages of recovery from the same type of surgery. I couldn't believe there were so many other kids in the same city, with the same disease as me, but there they were, filling the beds that lined the walls, as far as the eye could see.

I was fitted with a metal brace that extended from my neck to pelvis, with a specially contoured pelvic girdle and neck ring that was connected by metal bars in the front and back, so that I was forced to remain in an unnatural, straightened position…for 23 hours a day! And then they released me.

I left that sterile world where everyone was in the same boat, and thrust back into my own, where I was the only one. It was a nightmare beyond any I could have ever imagined; not only trying to do routine daily activities in the confines of that contraption and the physical pain that went along with it; and then of course having to deal with the kids at school who called me names and treated my like a freak. There was no preferential treatment from my parents or teachers, no counseling, nothing; just me against the world, for the next 8 years. Eventually I graduated from the medieval torture device to a less invasive one that I could wear under my clothes, but still I was a prisoner.

I'm now a grown man with two boys of my own and still suffering back pain on a daily basis. When I look at my children I can't even conceive the notion of jumping into such a serious situation as blind as my parents were, without any consideration of the physical and psychological ramifications. Looking back and realizing how technologically advanced our society has become, I still cannot help but wonder if the entire experience wasn't some sort of experiment disguised as good medicine. Perhaps I should start a support group…

Pepsi, Chips and a $5 Whore

I saw her hovering beside the dumpster when I pulled in the lot, and couldn't help but wonder if perhaps she'd just crawled out of it. She obviously hadn't bathed in days, possibly weeks. Her clothes were torn and covered in filth, and the open sores on her arms were in desperate need of medical attention.

I saw him when I went inside to buy a pack of smokes; just an average Joe, buying a bottle of Pepsi and a bag of chips. He paid, asked for two fives instead of a ten then left the store. I didn't give him a second glance; until I walked out and saw him conversing with the girl at the dumpster. Not sure who propositioned who, but she smiled her rotten-toothed grin and hopped in the truck beside him. I refused to turn away, when he looked around to see if anyone was watching and met my scrutinizing gaze. I saw shame cross his face momentarily; and ashamed he should have been!

This gives the term dumpster-diving a whole new meaning for me.

I cannot believe, in this day and age, that someone would be so hard-up for an orgasm that they would stoop to such depths of desperation to achieve it. Now, I don't know what exactly he had in mind, but I cannot even fathom being a man and putting my willy in a dirty mouth filled with rotten teeth, if in fact that was the intended orifice…ok, I'm making myself sick now…but you're following me, right?

Call me naïve, but when I think of prostitution, I imagine old-time brothels with painted ladies in lacy dresses with petticoats; breasts trimmed in lace and taffeta, rugged cowboys in boots and leather chaps, smelling like the trail and ready to unwind; beautiful babes in designer duds, catering to even more beautiful men of wealth and power, finding mutual stimulation and satisfaction, followed by the exchange of several crisp hundred dollar bills at the end of the evening.

I know…I know…I live in a world of fiction and fantasy and tend to romanticize everything, but still. What I witnessed made me sick to my stomach and little bit sad. Sad for both of them actually; and while I know I shouldn't judge, sometimes I still do.

Decadence

I went in looking to dig up some dirt on the old man and ended up falling in love. It wasn't just luck that landed me a spot on the landscaping crew, but months of preparation and hobnobbing; knowing full well that by being outdoors I'd have a better vantage point, in order to watch the comings and goings of the mansion. I also knew that all he had to do was be at the right place at the right time to find me there, and that's exactly what happened.

I'd been on the job for three weeks when out of the blue I was summoned inside. And so with grass stained kakis, unruly curls bellowing in the breeze and a smudge of dirt on the side of my face, I made my way across the lawn toward the mansion; as he stood in the upstairs window and watched me make my way.

I took off my boots at the door and trod barefoot across the marble floor, as I was led to a sitting room where I was instructed to wait. So far I hadn't seen anything out of the ordinary, except for the four scantly clad, non-blondes I passed, making their way from the breakfast buffet up the stairs, to where I assumed their rooms were. They were young, gorgeous and very friendly, but I don't believe they were whores. In fact, according to the picture gracing the mantle, I'd have to say they were his girlfriends.

And just as I turned from the portrait, there he was, standing just inside the door smiling at me. He was very matter-of-fact, as he walked confidently across the room and told me that while I looked lovely in his garden, it was his desire to pluck me out of there and add me to his bouquet of beauties; explaining that all my wishes would come true, inside these walls, if I chose to dwell with him. And I was prepared to do just that, while keeping in close contact with my team on the outside, who patiently awaited my signal for the bust; a signal that would never come.

What I found was not a sleazy pimp, as many believed him to be, but instead, a lonely, aging, insecure man, who had made his fortune by showcasing beautiful, uninhibited women; paving the way to fame for some, while nurturing and caring personally for others. And he did care, deeply; for each and every one of his girls. And now I was to be one of them.

He had a way about him; suave, debonair and somewhat arrogant, in a boyish sort of way and while we never engaged in any sexual activity, the hours spent alone in his company, talking and pondering the world, opened a place in my heart, that he silently slipped into and stole.

He was charming and sincere, offering a chance at a better life than what the streets had to give these girls, many of which he'd saved from just that; but my people didn't believe, didn't want to hear that the girls were there of their own free will, as it was easier to play the cynic and believe something illegal had to be going on.

I stayed with him for 9 months, and in that time I was introduced to a world of decadence that I had never even allowed myself to dream of. I came away with an appreciation for life and a better understanding of my self. For this man was not a sinner, but a saint; who forced a person to see the good inside themselves; the good in this sometimes rotten world we live, and release the negative demons that would otherwise drag us down.

My only regret was the way he found out my true identity, and that I wasn't merely a beautiful flower that he'd come upon in his garden, but a bug that had purposely been planted, among all that beauty he'd worked so hard to cultivate.

The disappointment was evident on his face and in his eyes, when they came and took me away. And although I never had a chance to tell him how sorry I was, or how much he had changed my life, I have to believe that somewhere, deep inside, he knew this truth about me. And maybe, just maybe, he remembers our time together and thinks of me with a smile.

I know I do.

Worst Job

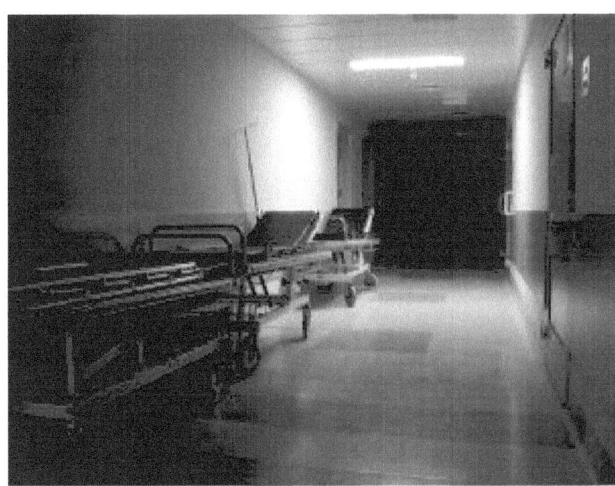

I stood in her darkened bathroom with the window cracked, looking out over S.R. 32 listening to the Friday night traffic, and still I could hear her breathing through the door. The night autumn air was cool on my face, as I leaned against the sill wishing myself away; anywhere but there would do.

She was dying, in constant pain, as the cancer ate away at her bones, and I was left to tend her alone. I knew she had to be changed, the urine so strong it stung my eyes the minute I entered the room, but this was a task that I dreaded more than anything. So, I tried to be quick about it, as I rolled her over, wiped her bottom, riddled with bedsores and rolled up the soiled cotton square, placing another in its place before rolling her back over the mountain of cloth and moving to the other side of the bed to repeat the process.

I knew it hurt her when I did this, but in my mind, my young, nineteen-year-old mind, the one loud groan of pain as I quickly performed the task at hand, was better than the drawn out agony she suffered when I took my time; either way it was horrible…for both of us.

Then one night, as I worked my way, down that long dark hall of souls, her room being at the end and the last on my rounds, I entered, only to find that the room was empty; her bed neatly made, the vase of plastic flowers that sat on her bedside table gone, and no stinging smell of urine.

I left my cart outside the door, walked to the bathroom and opened the window wide, deeply breathing in the cool night air, and in the secret depths of my heart, was glad that she had passed.

My training had consisted of following another nursing attendant around for one week before I was left alone on the skilled nursing floor. It was the worst job I ever had and twenty plus years later, I sometimes wake from a sound sleep; hearing her moans that linger in the depths of my mind, seeing here there in my mind's eye, her rigid body and gnarled fingers reaching out as I turn her over; and each time this happens, I ask for forgiveness for any unnecessary pain I may have caused this intimate stranger, in her final months of life.

Penetrating the Veil

They say the eyes are the windows of the soul and I believe this to be true. However, there are some who wear a veil over these windows and seeing inside is nearly impossible. I don't know how or why, but over time I've been given a gift that allows me to see, through a rare and finely-tuned lens, the life force that burns within certain people I encounter; a lens that forces me to see through the façade that many hide behind, exposing their true nature, which often times leaves me feeling like I've been cursed, rather than gifted.

The first time it happened I was sitting in a drive-thru waiting for my food. The girl at the window was young, pretty and polite. She took my money and waited while the food was being prepared and suddenly the bright aura she resonated began to fade to gray, as a young man approached her. I watched him, unable to look him in the eye, as his sole focus was on her and her alone.

He stood beside her, fiddling with napkins or some such thing, obviously an excuse to be close; a genuine feeling of fear and dread building inside me, as I watched, unnoticed. As she handed me my food through the window, I said, "You need to watch out and be careful of that one," as I nodded in his direction. She turned, looked over her shoulder then back to me and rolled her eyes, as if she knew exactly what I was talking about. And while she may have been aware of his lingering presence in all its creepiness, she apparently had no idea that my warning was literal; as three weeks later the news reported the arrest of twenty-two year old, Jeremy Lancaster, for the rape and brutal murder of his co-worker.

I'm seeing something now that leaves me torn; torn between confessing my suspicions or simply ignoring them.

I'd only seen him in the pictures that grace her desk, but his image alone was enough to send chills down my spine. She'd talked to me once about his incessant need for sex and her women's prayer group touching on the subject; leaving her to believe that it's the responsibility of the wife to submit to the husband in all aspects of life, regardless of her own feelings, needs and desires.

"They told me if I don't keep him satisfied that he'll just go out and find someone who will, and then it'll be my fault for not doing everything in my power to keep my marriage intact." Needless to say, I was stunned and outraged, but being familiar with the beliefs and teachings of some southern religions, I kept my mouth shut, knowing full well that anything I had to say would either go in one ear and out the other, or right over her head.

Then it happed, completely unexpected; his true essence exposed, revealing what a sick bastard he truly is.

We were at a company picnic and had meandered down to the beach, when she came walking up to introduce me to her husband and two beautiful daughters. The girls were polite and very well mannered, just as I had expected them to be, but when she introduced me to her husband, even though he shook my hand, he refused to look me in the eye, which was no surprise.

I watched him then, watching his girls as they talked to their mother; watched as his eyes lingered over the slender figure of the teenager as she took off her clothes to go swimming in the ocean. Watched as he rested his hands on her shoulders and his finger gently caressed the softness of her neck while he unhooked her necklace, his gaze becoming distant and consumed; to the point that when my husband asked what he did for a living, he didn't even hear him. He turned and watched as they made their way to the waters edge, as the unnatural urge built inside and beckoned him to her, and within minutes he had her over his shoulder, as he ran toward the waves and they both disappeared under the water.

I was totally and completely enthralled, unable to tear my gaze away as they broke the surface and he pulled her into his arms, causing her to squeal in delight, as her daddy picked her up and threw her into the next oncoming wave. Then I looked at the mother, who was watching them also, and when she turned and I saw the look on her face, I knew that she was completely aware, but too weak and insecure to do anything about it, and then I became incensed; wondering what the church ladies would have to say about this, once it comes to light, which I have absolutely no doubt will in time!

Alone

How attractive he was, when life is what I
feared and death was what I sought; until
the veil was lifted and I saw just how close
to the edge I was living; and suddenly
shifted. A newfound respect and
appreciation was ingrained in my soul and
suddenly happiness and love were all that
mattered; two things he was incapable of
giving and refused to accept.

Years of abuse that wore me down, until I
was nothing more than a mere shadow of
my self, fearing that shadow as if I were
being stalked. Silently I prayed and pleaded
for strength, wanting out with nowhere to
go, while my sanity slipped away like the
tears from my eyes.

The plea was answered, strength and sanity restored, love and happiness
found; and while the memories still linger in the depths of my mind, they
only act as a reminder of the power of prayer and how faith and love can
raise and renew us, from even the bowels of hell.

Wicked

She opened her self to him, like never before had been done. The feeling of freedom in the release and sharing, she found to be overwhelming; allowing it to carry her away. How easily she was led astray, by his wicked games and fanciful notions; playing upon her deepest emotions. The sensations he stirred too powerful to be anything but real. He then closed the door to keep her at bay, so as not to be affected by the things she might say.

He was a coward.

It's not always about winning

But sometimes it sure helps…

We've been fortunate to be on the same team with the same wonderful coaches since Cole started playing baseball 3 years ago. November before last he suffered a severe break in his arm (not playing baseball), and wasn't able to make it to try-outs in January, because we were still waiting to see whether or not he was going to have to have surgery. Turns out he got drafted to another team, but in the end, coach traded two boys to get him back, not even knowing if he'd be ready to start training for spring season, so that gives you an idea of the bond they have.

They aren't little boys anymore and therefore aren't treated as such; the players are more aggressive and so are the coaches, cutting no slack whatsoever, and therein, I believe lies the problem. He doesn't respond well to yelling and screaming – it's not something he's accustomed to and therefore doesn't understand why people think that by raising their voice and becoming belligerent that the expected results will be attained any faster or better than if you just simply speak…but there again, yelling is part of the sport, so he needs to thicken his skin and deal with it, which he is, but still bitches about on occasion.

The last few games he's just been in a foul mood, not busting it like he should and making silly mistakes then beating himself up over it. It's disheartening to watch, but what are you gonna do, its something he has to work through himself, and tonight he did. Big time!

First time at bat he rips it to left field and makes a single. He then proceeds to steal second...seals third...and then SCORES!!! Second at bat he rips a line drive and gets a single...steals second then gets out at third.

They're ahead 6 -7, the other team is last at bat and we need to hold 'em, looking for three up, three down. The lights are on, it's starting to rain, the shower is soft and steady, but a little wet isn't going to stop these boys from kicking the Cubs' butts, or us from watching!

First batter up and Ashley strike's him out...second batter hits a double...third batter walks, forth batter strikes out. One more out and we take the game. Player on first, player on second, plays to first. Last kid at bat...the count is full and he rips it to left field, where my baby is baseball ready; takes three steps forward, glove out, eyes the size of saucers and takes it in the chest...right into his glove. His face beams, his arms shoot straight up over his head, the crowd screams, he does a little happy dance, I almost pee my pants and the whole team rushes and dog piles him! The coaches rushed the field, some of the parents rush the field and I stood there in the rain with my eyes welling over, listening to the team and the crowd cheering, *"COLE...COLE...COLE!!!"*

It was one of those priceless moments that I wouldn't trade for anything in the world! Not only did he walk away with the game ball, but his heart was overflowing once again, with his one true love...baseball.

Never Ending

So many things I could have said, insults I could have slung, as we stood face-to-face; her gaze scrutinizing me from head-to-toe; and I thought to my self, if only I were that kind of person.

Her smartass sneer told me that she hadn't yet let it go and the mere sight of me caused her angst, bringing the whole sordid affair rushing to the surface; an affair that has long since been swept away with the tide.

If given the opportunity, I would tell her that the man I briefly knew was nothing whatsoever, like the man she calls her husband, and that what we shared had absolutely nothing to do with her, or anyone else for that matter.

Some things cannot be explained or defined, they just are what they are, and we chose to explore instead of ignore, the spiritual, intellectual and sexual connection that we found in each other. And while it meant everything at the time and I wouldn't have missed it for the world, it is so deeply buried, that it would take multiple lifetimes to breach the surface once more.

I would also say that I am truly sorry; for the pain, anguish, self-doubt and mistrust that my selfish actions caused. However, it is quite clear that what I prophesied has come to fruition, and the affair was, in fact, the best thing that could have happened to their marriage. For they *are* still together, and perhaps she no longer takes for granted, the man who shares her world; knowing beyond a doubt that all could be lost so easily.

Perhaps now, her complacency is at bay and the words come more easily, as I can attest he longs to hear. And just maybe, her focus has shifted, and the spotlight is once again shining down on him; for as livid and disgusted as she was with him, her fear ran twice as deep.

Chances are though, even in all my sincerity, she wouldn't believe a word I said, and I can't say that I blame her; as I'll always be viewed as a threat in her eyes, and rightfully so I suppose; in which case I'd end the conversation with a few suggestions on technique, that I personally know drives him wild. If only I were that kind of person.

Someday Sunday

Cool air wafts through the windows, stirring remnants of impure thoughts that linger in her mind; lace curtains billowing, as if they'd come to life. Ancient limbs tangled with vines, Spanish moss like dirty cobwebs; lifeless, reflecting her mood and the gray of the darkened sky. Waiting for the rain, so as to wash her sin, completely away.

The room where he lays

She stood at the base of the stairs looking up, her fear and uncertainty nearly overwhelming. The forth step creaking causing her to pause, as she momentarily considered turning back, the thought of being so close urging her on.

She walked softly down the hall, stopping in the doorway of the room where he lay; a light outside the window, perhaps the glow of the moon illuminating the room, giving it a bluish hue. His back was toward the door, curled slightly fetal on his left side; his dark hair, a striking contrast against the pale pillow. The outline of his body under the blanket was all of him she could see.

She stood for several minutes, watching him sleep; taking in what details she could, her focus coming back to the curved headboard; images of him grasping the rails, as he made love to whoever it was he took to his bed.

He knew the moment she entered the room, heard the muffled sound as her clothes hit the floor. She crawled in behind him, feeling his heat; two spoons in a drawer, and still he didn't move; nor did he push her away when she put her arm around him, in an attempt to ease his pain.

Satan's Lobotomy

I talked till I was blue in the face, believing that I'd finally reached her and she was going to do the right thing; by moving back home and making amends with her ex-husband, in an attempt to once again be a mother to her children, whom she'd been relieved of all parental rights, for reasons I can only imagine.

I didn't want to be her friend, as she just wasn't my kind of people, but I was on this forgiveness and love thy neighbor kick and thought it was the Christian thing to do. Plus, if there was anything I could do to reunite a mother and her children, then I felt good and was certain I was doing the right thing.

She called me several times after she moved back and it sounded like she was finally getting her act together, then the calls stopped coming altogether. I wanted to believe it was because she was spending so much time with her kids and finally living a normal, happy and healthy life, but this couldn't be further from the truth.

She showed up on my doorstep a week ago, nearly a year to the day since she'd left, and I swear I didn't recognize her, nor did I have a clue as to the identify of the creepy, greasy man that she brought with her. I stood there, my mouth agape, when her voice rang familiar and it finally registered, after she told me who she was.

I'd heard of this monster, the man-made one, whose euphoric rush, which some describe as the equivalent of 10 orgasms, lasting anywhere from 5 to 30 minutes, triggers an explosive release of dopamine in the pleasure center of the brain; causing the user to feel aggressively smarter and unstoppable, only to be returned to a state slightly deteriorated of that from whence they came. But until now, I had no idea of the devastation and havoc it can wreak on a human being.

She looked like an old woman, 90 lbs. at most, whose face was covered with open sores and the few teeth remaining, slowly rotting out of her head. She needed a place to crash and wash up before heading back out. They were on their way to Miami, running from the law; the FBI specifically. All said with a smile and amusement.

I wondered if it was the truth or some fantastic delusion brought on by the drugs and brain damage she'd obviously sustained. It didn't matter one way or the other, as I shut the door in her face and rang the police 40 minutes later to come pick up the couple passed out on my front lawn.

WARNING
Methamphetamine destroys…PERIOD. Don't do it, not even once!

Inoubliable vous

Shrouded in mystery
Hiding behind the veil
Uncompromising position
Never giving in

So thin at times
Thought she saw inside
A glimpse of his reality
Buried within the illusion

Illusions can be grand
He whispered softly
Turning out the light
Taking her by the hand

Wordsmith Extraordinaire

Friday night
Open mic
Out on the deck
New Orleans Café

Never been one
For public displays
Even at book signings
The attention I don't dig

But the air was abuzz
My mind just right
To be quite frank
I had something to say

So I took the stage
Mic in hand
Closed my eyes
Let it rip

The crowd went wild
I tossed a handful of cards
Took my leave
As they begged for more

Infamy

He had her so tightly wound she couldn't tell where he ended and she began; emotions constantly soaring to endless heights of infinity, not caring if she ever came down. His truth she refused to believe, even when it was so plain to see; wondering how long they'd live this life of lies, holding back the question, wanting to know why. Then it all came crashing down. World without end. Amen…amen; and still she couldn't stay away.

Tall wrought iron gates, road canopied and lined with trees; this way she's forced to travel, to reach the place where now he lays. On the crest of a knoll, at the edge of the woods; the sound of the brook and a picturesque view of the mansion on the hill. She went seeking solace, searching for him, talking out loud, cries carried on the wind; sitting for hours, numb with grief, lying on his grave wishing for death to steal her away. Too frightened to do it herself.

Death did not find her. Satan's spawn however, did; on that warm summer day, the smell of fresh-cut grass filling her senses as she made her way through the gate. Daisies in hand to fill the vase; the sound of the mower distant and far away, growing louder much too quickly; paying little attention, until he called her name.

She turned from her perch atop the tomb, to find him just a few feet away; pants pulled down, member in hand, crazed look in his eye as he flopped it around. Her heart jumped in her throat and hammered violently, as she took off running, several hundred yards to her car; he chased after, screaming for her to stop. He banged the window as she fumbled for her keys, nearly running him over as she escaped unscathed; hysterical she headed straight for the police.

The court date came; he was wearing a suit, two sizes too big, obviously borrowed. He denied of course but lost his job anyway. She was mortified, humiliated, filled with shame and rage; infamy would soon closely follow her name; when she took the stand and the first thing they said, "Describe for us in detail, exactly what your were wearing that day…"

Return to Me

The light of day is not yet seen, she feels him wandering inside her dreams. He touches her softly, he whispers sweet words; it's been so long since his voice was heard. Yet she feels him, as many times before, as he enters quietly through her minds door.

Friday Night Scrimmage

Cool air
Slight drizzle
Sun setting
Lights shining
Bats cracking
Gnats biting
Gloves smacking
Dragonflies mating
Boys laughing
Dirt flying
Coaches signaling
Crowd cheering

Mirror, Mirror on the Wall

She didn't see what others saw when she studied her reflection in the looking glass. Her face was the same, but for what time had changed, and although no one ever guessed correctly, still, *she* knew her true age. Nothing but a number; she'd believed that all her life, until she crossed the line. Closer now to the finish whilst looking ahead, then she was to the start looking back. That frightened her; her mortality; and so many things still left undone. Things that were lost and yet to be found; searching for answers while losing sight of the questions.

She'd used her looks to get just about anything she wanted, choosing more wisely as comes only with age, but what happens when they fail her? What would become of her then? Will they look in her eyes that once sparkled like gems and see the wisdom she'd gathered over the years that she'd lived, or dull green eyes having lost their shine? Would her words and stories mean near as much, if her image in the sidebar were to suddenly change; silver flecks now framing her face. Are they really so shallow and superficial, or is it simply her skewed vision of her self, ability and worth.

Why do they come here? What is it they seek? A bit of fantasy perhaps that she gives so freely? Pieces of her self for public viewing; never knowing for certain what is real or imaginary. An entertainer on stage for all the world to see; removing her clothes or sharing her prose. Is there a difference? Not really. And in the end, does it really matter what anyone thinks; or the importance being the truth of her self that she knows and accepts.

Fearless

On the spur of the moment she decided some pampering was in order, so she donned her favorite jeans and leather flip-flops, drove thru the bank, made a quick withdraw and headed to the spa for the full treatment; mani, pedi, tan and full-body massage. A few hours later she left feeling like a million bucks; with a spring in her step and money left to burn.

She headed toward the city, planning to stop and shop in San Marco for a while, but her plans took a quick turn when she was stopped at a light and saw him get off the bus. He was young, tan, well toned and knew it. The minute he hit the pavement he reached down and peeled the shirt up and over his head, his back and shoulder muscles rippling in the hot sun; her mouth watering as she watched. She knew in that instant there were only two choices; stop and inquire, or drive on and never know.

The light turned green and she flipped her blinker, making an immediate right and stopping short, with him just a few feet from the passenger door. He looked up, made eye contact and smiled. She rolled down the window and asked if he needed a ride. He hopped in, reclined the seat just a tad, thanked her, asked her name and where she was headed, to which she shook her and replied, "They'll be no more words."

They drove in silence, he lighting a cigarette and playing with the radio; selecting a station she never would have listened to but somehow fitting to the mood. They drove a few miles more, passing familiar landmarks that were nothing but a blur to her, before she pulled into the nearest hotel and booked a room.

Hours later, satiated and broke, she felt a fearlessness she'd never before known. The young stud was her first one bought; but after the hours they spent, she doubted he'd be the last.

Just Cause

It was all rather anti-climactic; the way he stood against the wall without touching her; his moans and heavy breathing the only telltale signs he was actually enjoying it. Slightly whorish, considering the position she'd assumed, but she wanted it just as much as he; she'd had her eye on him for quite some time, and although he wanted to do her first, she refused, as that just wasn't the way she'd imagined it. Still, some semblance of intimacy must be required if a girl is expected to take pleasure in giving; fingers tangled in hair, a soft caress on the cheek, or perhaps the tracing of lips with fingertips; but what did she expect, they *were* occupying a stall in the women's room at the tavern, two days before her wedding, when her best friend entered innocently and caught them.

*And if anyone here has just cause why this couple should not be joined in holy matrimony, let them speak now or forever hold their peace…*She held her tongue as she watched the happy couple climb atop the carriage; rented horse, rented tux, custom-made Cinderella dress and lifetime of lies ahead of them.

Woman-girl

"Come sit with me," he said, easing back onto the couch, watching her walk across the room. She could feel his eyes caressing, taking in her every move, causing self-consciousness to flood her senses, to the point that she was unable to look at him, for fear she would say or do something to ruin the moment.

He thought she was perfect.

She sat down beside him, not wanting to sit too close, or be too far away. With a shaky hand she took the wine he offered, sipped and smiled, trying hard not to wince at the sweet tartness, as he silently mused at her inexperience. After only half a glass she could feel the warmth flowing through her body and began to relax.

She was young, shy and innocent; clearly not used to being in the company of men and although he wanted her more than anything, he knew savoring her until the moment was right would be absolute bliss; pushing her to the edge until she begged him to take her.

"You're so beautiful," he whispered; reaching out and brushing the hair from her eyes; eyes filled with innocence, hunger, yearning and fear. She dropped her gaze and lowered her head, clearly embarrassed by his words. He gently touched her chin with his finger, slowly raising her face until she was looking at him and he once again had her full attention.

"You are…" he leaned in, barely touching his lips to hers.
"So…" he breathed the word into her mouth; his breath hot on her flesh, lingering now on her cheek. "Beautiful…" he whispered in her ear, opened his mouth and suckled her neck, slowly cupping her face in his hands, capturing her mouth with his.

She'd never been kissed with such tender passion; never felt so special and wanted; sensing the moments end coming, she reached up in one bold gesture, ran her hands through his hair and pulled him closer – her tongue exploring wildly, passion igniting inside her – instinct taking over as she leaned back slowly and pulled him down on top of her.

Her body was flooded with sensations she'd never before known, as her want and desire grew with each delicate caress; moments passing too quickly, her mind willing time to stop. The heat that radiated from within, slowly driving her mad; feeling the weight of him on top of her, as he pressed himself closer, rubbing his hardness against her, until she thought she'd burn up inside if he didn't touch her.

She let her hands roam freely, taking in every inch of his body; drowning slowly in her own desire. He ran his hand along her hip, up the side of her body, teasingly brushing against her breast, lingering, unmoving. She let out a little cry as he cupped it in his hand, gently squeezed as she squirmed beneath him, suddenly raising her hips to meet him.

He cradled her in his arm, rising above until he was looking down into her sultry wanton eyes, then slowly he thrust himself against her. Fascinated by her response; her eyes closed, lips parted, her movements matched his stroke-for-stroke. Her sweet young body trembling beneath his.

She moaned and he pulled her closer, letting her grind against him, until her breathing became labored and he eased her back down; his hand roaming downward between her breasts, lingering over her belly, coming to rest where he knew she wanted it; feeling her heat as he rested his palm there, increasing the pressure just a bit; smiling to himself when she arched her back and raised her hips, pressing hard against his hand; a teardrop running down her cheek, her bottom lip quivering.

God, she was so fucking precious. He could only imagine how sweet it would be when he finally made her his. For now though, it was enough to simply watch her reaction, as he touched her through a layer of clothing; her countenance revealing everything she was feeling. A woman-girl if ever there was one.

Alejandro

Dark witted candor I came oh, so familiar
From whence his verve doeth stem
Fashioned play on words, intellectual terms
His mentor he hath studied well

Of human condition with keen perception
Explorer of frenzied minds
Searching for answers without any questions
Fiddler of reason and rhyme

Malicious intent swarming inside
Begging to be let out
Vile attempts at humor, distasteful amusement
Taking pleasure in showing contempt

Tormented by demons of others, his own
Behind this mask he does hide
Afraid to show face, unveil his disgrace
Embracing exiles restraints

Keep reaching out he withdraws even more
Making you feel the fool
Worry and wonder, lust and desire
Feeling exactly the way he wants –

Compose

She was flooded with a myriad of emotions, as she sat down to compose the letter; knowing full well that this would be their final contact. Her last chance to say all the things needing to be said, expressing what he had meant to her. She suddenly longed for the days when everything between them was understood and felt. Without words. When time stood still. The universe was in perfect balance. The earth moved, with the two of them connected at its core. Twin flames uniting into one beautiful and perfect whole.

B o u n d a r i e s

Feeling fine
Probing begins
Opened my self
Emotional distress

Wanted to know
Let him ask
Answered honestly
No bullshit allowed

Questioning again
Past mistakes
Digging up shit
Wishing I hadn't –

About the Author

Jill describes herself as a word-weaver, story teller, truth-seeker; who finds solace in putting her thoughts to words and sharing with all those who would listen. An accomplished award winning author, whose talents span several genres; Jill is one of those people who have found what she loves to do and keeps plugging away, despite the odds.

A genuine love of the craft and a satisfying creative outlet is what keeps her turning out one book after another. Her natural ability to light a fire of compassion as well as heart-pounding excitement has been extolled time and again by reviewers and readers alike.

All books are written under pen name J.A. Terry and are available wherever books are sold. For more information, visit her website at jillterry.com. For a list of upcoming releases, visit www.pandorasboox.org.

Other titles by Jill Terry:

Time Passages

Exposed

Full Circle

MACUMBA

Shadows of my Soul

Premonition

Destination Unknown

Anthologies:

Coffee Break Poetry

Unrestrained

Pandora's Boox

Filling the Box - One Story at a Time...

www.pandorasboox.org

www.ingramcontent.com/pod-product-compliance
Lightning Source LLC
Chambersburg PA
CBHW030526030726
47495CB00004B/872